GUILTY

The Shooting Script
The Waking Nightmare
The Past Tense
The Dead Letter
The Double Life
The Last Word

The Monk Series
Mr. Monk Goes to the Firehouse
Mr. Monk Goes to Hawaii
Mr. Monk and the Blue Flu
Mr. Monk and the Two Assistants
Mr. Monk in Outer Space
Mr. Monk Goes to Germany
Mr. Monk Is Miserable
Mr. Monk and the Dirty Cop
Mr. Monk in Trouble
Mr. Monk Is Cleaned Out
Mr. Monk on the Road
Mr. Monk on the Couch
Mr. Monk on Patrol
Mr. Monk Is a Mess
Mr. Monk Gets Even

The Charlie Willis Series
My Gun Has Bullets
Dead Space

The Dead Man Series (coauthored with William Rabkin)
Face of Evil
Ring of Knives (with James Daniels)
Hell in Heaven
The Dead Woman (with David McAfee)
The Blood Mesa (with James Reasoner)

Kill Them All (with Harry Shannon)
The Beast Within (with James Daniels)
Fire & Ice (with Jude Hardin)
Carnival of Death (with Bill Crider)
Freaks Must Die (with Joel Goldman)
Slaves to Evil (with Lisa Klink)
The Midnight Special (with Phoef Sutton)
The Death March (with Christa Faust)
The Black Death (with Aric Davis)
The Killing Floor (with David Tully)
Colder Than Hell (with Anthony Neil Smith)
Evil to Burn (with Lisa Klink)
Streets of Blood (with Barry Napier)
Crucible of Fire (with Mel Odom)
The Dark Need (with Stant Litore)
The Rising Dead (with Stella Green)
Reborn (with Kate Danley, Phoef Sutton, and Lisa Klink)

The Jury Series
Judgment (aka .357 Vigilante #1)
Adjourned (aka .357 Vigilante #2: Make Them Pay)
Payback (aka .357 Vigilante #3: White Wash)
Guilty (aka .357 Vigilante #4: Killstorm)

Nonfiction
The Best TV Shows You Never Saw
Unsold Television Pilots 1955–1989
Television Fast Forward
Science Fiction Filmmaking in the 1980s (cowritten with
William Rabkin, Randy Lofficier, and Jean-Marc Lofficier)
*The Dreamweavers: Interviews with Fantasy
Filmmakers of the 1980s* (cowritten with William
Rabkin, Randy Lofficier, and Jean-Marc Lofficier)
Successful Television Writing (cowritten with William Rabkin)

GUILTY

LEE GOLDBERG

Published by
Cutting Edge Books
PO Box 8212
Calabasas, CA 91372
www.cuttingedgebooks.com

PROLOGUE

Los Angeles
Sunday, June 9, 2:45 p.m.

The pigeon did a Charlie Chaplin waddle and dropped dead on the man's shiny black shoe. The man kicked it away, startling a few of the other birds around his park bench into flight.

He reached into the pocket of his Brooks Brothers jacket for another Alka-Seltzer, tore open the wrapper, and began breaking the tablet into tiny pieces. A lazy Sunday in the park spent feeding the birds. He had forgotten how nice it could feel.

He tossed the Alka-Seltzer bits to the birds and dipped into his pocket for another tablet. Rays of sunlight filtered through the smog and ricocheted off the man-made lake into the reflective lenses of his aviators. Sweat glistened on his blunt, wide brow, and his skin itched under his gray pin-striped suit. He examined the palms of his hands, powdered white from the antacid, and ignored the two birds rattling on the pavement. He didn't ignore the bag lady.

The old woman was approaching from his left and pushing a rusted grocery cart that looked like it had been dredged up from the bottom of the ocean. The wire cage was bulging with brown bags overstuffed with newspapers, ratty clothes, and crushed aluminum cans. The woman was hunched over the cart, her leathery face staring into the bags as if she saw something there besides trash.

The woman parked her cart against the bench and sat down heavily beside the man. She smelled like a bucket full of old rainwater, and her face looked like a rotting apple.

"What are you up to?" the woman asked in a ragged breath nearly drowned by mucus.

"Killing time."

"That's my job." Her voice was smooth and soft this time, betraying youth. The man broke up another Alka-Seltzer in his hands and threw it to the tottering birds mirrored in his sunglasses.

"We have a job for you." He clapped his hands against each other to wipe off the powder and removed a manila envelope from the inside pocket of his jacket. He handed it to her without turning to look at her.

The woman set the envelope on her lap and opened the flap. Inside, she found six sheets of typewritten paper and six black-and-white photographs. A bird fluttered in the air, screeched, and dropped onto the bench between them.

She regarded the dead bird with a sideways glance and saw the Alka-Seltzer wrappers around the man's feet.

"Pigeons don't belch," the man said, watching the birds peck at the Alka-Seltzer bits. "Their stomachs just blow up."

She carefully slid the papers back into the envelope.

"My fee is a million dollars," she said.

"We've already wired the funds into the designated Swiss account."

"If you put a spring inside a piece of meat and toss it to a dog, he'll swallow it whole," she remarked casually, "and then scratch his stomach until he tears himself open."

The man smiled appreciatively.

She carefully sealed the clasp and slid the envelope between the slats of her shopping cart. "Why do you want me to kill a bunch of ordinary people?"

He rose to his feet with his back to her. "Brett Macklin is no ordinary man." He kicked a convulsing bird from his path and walked away.

❧   ❧   ❧

Puerto Vallarta, Mexico
Monday, June 10, 3:37 p.m.

Mort Suderson would drink motor oil as long as they served it to him in a coconut. It was exotic touches like using coconut shells for glasses that made Puerto Vallarta so wonderful to him. He dog-paddled away from the hotel's palapa-covered poolside bar and merrily sipped away, oblivious to the chlorinated water spilling into his piña colada.

Swimming to the tile-rimmed island in the center of the pool, he paused, setting his coconut on the grass and squinting through the palm fronds at the emerald waters of Banderas Bay. *Sure beats the hell out of LA,* he thought, praising himself once again for coming down here to recuperate from his tongue surgery.

A white ferry, teeming with American tourists, chortled south towards the thatched huts and waterfalls on Yelapa, where yesterday a woman with sandbag knockers tried to sell Mort an iguana. He didn't buy the lizard, but he did eat five small tacos and had been backfiring more than his '76 Chevette ever since.

He looked away from the ferry, adjusted his Speedo briefs, and watched the waves steep and crash on the pebbled sands of Las Glorias Beach. The warm water crawled up the beach to a pile of horse droppings being sniffed by one of the mangy, wild dogs that had chased Mort off the beach that morning.

Mort took a sip of his piña colada and let his legs float up behind him. While his eyes panned over the women basking in chaise lounges around the pool, he kicked at the surface of the water, covering up the echoes of yesterday's tacos that emanated from his body.

His steady, traveling gaze moved unnoticed over oil-slicked backs and delicate buttocks, across sweat-dampened breasts and parched lips.

And then he felt her eyes on his back. Mort might have shrugged off the sensation, or reached back to swat off a nonexistent insect, or just ignored it. But he didn't.

He turned slowly, scanning the faces, and came to a jolting halt at a pair of radiant blue eyes—eyes that were staring straight into his. She was set against the bleached white of the Holiday Inn and seemed to move towards him, though she wasn't moving at all. She wore a black string bikini and sat on the pool's edge directly across from him, dangling her long, golden legs lazily in the water.

Grinning sheepishly, Mort picked up his drink and walked through the water towards her, contracting his pelvic muscles to jerk up his penis a little bit and give her something to dream about.

She watched him expressionlessly as he approached. She was dark, a Mediterranean, with cool eyes and sharp features, the kind of woman that used to scare him. They scared him because he wanted them but didn't think he could satisfy them.

That was before his operation. Now his tongue could work miracles. Now that woman could be his. He smoothed the beads of water off his chest to draw her eyes to it.

"Hey, *yo hablo* English?" Mort asked, doing his best Ricardo Montalban.

She regarded him for a long moment, during which his smile never wavered.

"Yes," she said wearily, closing her eyes and tilting her head back into the sun. Mort's gaze plummeted into her deep cleavage. He didn't need his pelvic contractions anymore.

"So you down here on your own?" Mort asked.

She sighed impatiently, unmoving. "Yes."

Many men would have quit there. Not him. Mort pulled himself up onto the deck beside her. "Ever seen *Kramer vs. Kramer*?"

"Yes," she said, raising her head and looking out at the bay.

"Most men are too busy being macho to admit this," he said, "but I cried during that movie—"

She stood up, the fluid motion interrupting him, and glided away with her back to him. Mort's open mouth narrowed into an angry grimace.

Frigid bitch, Mort thought. She could have known absolute ecstasy.

But he didn't turn away. He didn't slide back into the pool and paddle back to the bar. He was still watching her when she stopped, cast an aloof glance at him over her shoulder, and said, "Aren't you coming?"

Un-fucking-believable, absolutely un-fucking-believable.

It was every sex fantasy Mort ever had coming true—he sees a beautiful woman, their eyes meet, a few words are spoken, and then wham, they're in the sack, fucking each other silly.

Mort Suderson rested on his back, soaking the sheets with his sweat. She straddled him, moving herself gently up and down, her hands clutching his legs. He squeezed her breasts again to prove to himself that this was honest-to-God happening, that Mort Suderson was screwing perfection.

He always knew his life would be this way. He had faith. He kept believing. He didn't let the premature-ejaculation stuff or the impotence business get him down. No, he kept working at it. He got the right threads. He exuded the right attitude. He got the membrane snipped under his tongue.

He was granite, she was beautiful, and this was nearly heaven. They were burning the fucking sheets.

And now he would reward her.

"Lie down, baby," he moaned. "I'm gonna send you into outer space."

She lifted herself off of him and rolled onto her back beside him. Mort kissed her and let his hand glide between her warm, wet legs.

He stuck out his tongue at her. "See this?" he slobbered, pointing at his tongue with his index finger.

"Prepare yourself for the end-all, baby."

Mort pulled her by the hips to the end of the bed and stood on the floor, staring down at her. God, she was beautiful. She was smiling, but in a funny kind of way, like someone was whispering a joke to her that he couldn't hear. It didn't matter. He knew what her body was saying. Her eyes were closed, her stomach flat, her breasts firm and damp. He dropped to his knees, grinned, and spread her legs apart. He leaned forward and began probing and teasing her with his tongue.

Her body stiffened at his touch and she moaned, her legs closing around him. He took it as encouragement, flicking his tongue in rapid, light strokes. She rose into a sitting position, rested her hands on his head, and swayed pleasurably from side to side.

Her legs squeezed tighter, pinning his head in place. He sucked with increased ardor. Her fingers dug into his scalp. Mort put his hands on her thighs and gently tried to push them apart. He couldn't get air. She closed her legs even tighter, her breathing becoming ragged, a smile etching a crooked path across her face.

Mort squirmed, trying to stand, pounding his fists into her legs. She shuddered with ecstasy, gritted her teeth against the unbearable, joyous sensations, and jerked her pelvis sharply to one side. The snap of Mort's neck coincided with the thunderbolt of pleasure that left her trembling.

CHAPTER ONE

Los Angeles
Tuesday, June 11, 1:38 a.m.

The day had been the shits for Brett Macklin. His checks were bouncing at the bank and bills were clogging his mailbox. All the hours he had spent going through the books at his Blue Yonder Airways, his charter airline, didn't make things any better. In fact, they were getting steadily worse.

He was already a half hour late to pick up Jessica Mordente at the *Los Angeles Times* when his '59 Cadillac ran out of gas. Now, with $20 in his wallet, his savings account tapped, his girlfriend probably pissed, and night giving way to morning, he was stuck in the middle of downtown LA pumping his own goddamn gas.

The Chevron station was sandwiched between the dark, iron skeleton of an emerging high-rise and the Harbor Freeway off-ramp. The asphalt around the station was cracked and rippled, as if buckled by the tight squeeze. The streetlamp buzzed and flickered, the light being smothered by the surrounding darkness.

The porcine gas station attendant who was supposed to be washing Macklin's windshield was, instead, smearing the glass with the greasy shirt stretched over his stomach and ashes from his cigar. Macklin saw the name "Earl" embroidered on the man's bulging shirt pocket, smudged by oily fingerprints.

Macklin jerked his thumb at the big "NO SMOKING" sign over the gas pumps behind him. "Hey, Earl, can't you read your own sign? It's dangerous to smoke here."

Earl shrugged. "I like to live on the edge."

A white VW rabbit sputtered up on the other side of the pump island. A bespectacled teenager in corduroy shorts and a rugby shirt burst out of the car and dashed past them to the men's room.

Earl yelled, "The crapper's for customers only." But, it was wasted breath; the kid had already disappeared inside, leaving his VW shivering and choking.

"Shit, every whore and bum in town thinks that's their private crapper." Earl ambled over to Macklin and let his hand glide over the car, up over the teardrop-shaped cab and down along the sharp, arching fins. "Piss 'n' run, piss 'n' run. I gotta sell rubbers and dildos in there just so I can afford to clean up the place, you know?"

Earl leaned against the gas pump to Macklin's left, flicked his cigar, and stuck it between his plump lips. "Nice night, huh?"

"Oh yeah," Macklin groaned. "Nice night." He looked past Earl. The night trembled, like a movie when the film fails to catch on the projector's sprockets. The picture wasn't quite right. Macklin narrowed his eyes. A warm breeze blew scraps of paper across the deserted street like tumbleweeds. Then he saw the three blacks, illuminated in the lightning flash of the faulty streetlamp. One carried a bat, the others swung chains.

"A real nice night," Macklin muttered wearily.

He slowly turned to his right. Four more men peeled off from the darkness carrying crowbars and chains, led by a Michael Jackson clone. The gang leader wore reflective sunglasses, a white sequined glove, and a broad-shouldered red jacket Macklin guessed had been stolen off the doorman at the Westwood Marquis.

Earl followed Macklin's gaze and his eyes bulged with fear. "Th-The Bloodhawks," he stammered. The seven Bloodhawks formed a loose circle around the property.

Macklin kept pumping his gas.

Michael Jackson, bobbing to the beat of a private song, grinned and dismissed the station with his gloved hand. "Trash it," he said.

The three gang members behind Michael Jackson strolled up to the building, appraised it for a moment, and then smashed the windows out with their crowbars. The Bloodhawks spilled into the office. They bashed the shelves off the wall, whacked apart the candy machine, and tossed the desk into the street.

A black GI Joe wearing a beret and army fatigues strutted to the Sparkletts water cooler and swung his crowbar at the glass bottle. It exploded aqua blue, splashing the walls with water and glass.

At that moment, the teenager in shorts emerged from the bathroom. Before Macklin could react, GI Joe whirled, swinging at the teenager's head like it was another Sparkletts bottle. His skull broke like pottery and his body slapped against the wet wall, splattering it red.

"You're next, motherfucker." The Michael Jackson clone pointed a sequined finger at Macklin. "I've seen your fucking hearse before. You're the dogshit that's been coming onto our turf and kicking ass."

Macklin shrugged.

Michael Jackson whipped a switchblade from his back pocket and waved it in front of Macklin's impassive face. "Motherfucker, you're dead."

Macklin yanked the gas nozzle from his car and swung it in front Michael Jackson, spraying him with fuel. The man recoiled, spat, and charged blindly towards Macklin, who grabbed the cigar from Earl's mouth and tossed it at him.

Michael Jackson burst into flame. Shrieking with agony, he did a skittish moonwalk and tripped over his burning feet. He hit the ground rolling, screaming as he tried to smother the fire that consumed his body.

The gang members let out angry cries and ran at Macklin with their weapons raised. Macklin casually pulled the .357 Magnum from under his jacket and cocked it. Killing was becoming a reflex.

"Would anyone here like some .357 dental work?" he asked.

The men closing in on either side of him froze. The acrid stench of burned flesh filled the air. The only sound was the gang leader, crackling and bubbling.

"You can't kill us all," a gang member said defiantly.

Macklin shrugged. "Maybe it's my lucky day."

There was a long moment of indecision. Macklin could hear Earl's labored, anxious breaths.

"This isn't over, asshole," GI Joe hissed, holding his bloody crowbar out like a sword.

"It is for you." Macklin shot him. The bullet punched GI Joe in the chest and tossed him back onto the flaming corpse. GI Joe's crowbar clattered on the pavement.

Macklin sighed. "Who's next?"

The gang members looked at one another. They reached an unspoken agreement and suddenly scattered, leaving their two friends smoldering on the pavement.

Macklin holstered his gun, stuffed a crumpled $20 bill in Earl's breast pocket, and got into his car.

He started the engine and smiled through the open window at Earl's pale face.

"I like to live on the edge."

2:00 a.m.

"Being a vigilante is costing me a fortune," Brett Macklin said, his voice echoing off the bathroom walls. He sat on his toilet eating his double bacon chili cheeseburger and watching Jessica Mordente's naked body through the shower's frosted glass door.

"While I'm out on the streets, my airline business is going to hell. Things are even worse now that Mort, my only pilot, is down in Mexico." He slurped on his chocolate shake and set it on the toilet tank behind him. "Christ, do you know how much bullets cost?"

"So quit." Jessica scrubbed her shoulders with her Buf-Puf. "Go back to being a normal human being again." Steam spilled out of the shower stall and fogged the bathroom mirrors.

It's too late, Macky boy. It's a part of you now.

Macklin held the burger tightly in his hands and took a big bite. A glob of chili spurted out between the buns and dribbled down his shirt.

You can never go back, never…

Mordente pressed herself against the door and peered over the top at Macklin. "I didn't hear your clever retort."

He shrugged. His mouth was full.

She groaned melodramatically and turned away, letting the hot water beat against her chest. She luxuriated in the warm water, and Macklin, staring blankly at the floor, ate his Fatburger. The only sounds were the rushing water and the whirring fan.

"Have you heard of the Transformational Awareness Life Church?" she asked.

"That isn't the answer. I won't join." He swallowed his mouthful of food. "I don't want to become one of those EST-holes."

"I don't want you to join, and it isn't EST," she said. "I'm doing a story on them. It's one of those self-awareness, self-realization programs. A guy named Fraser Nebbins runs it. They have their own little community out in the desert."

"Yeah, so what's the story? There's dozens of weirdo groups like that in Los Angeles. They franchise them like McDonald's. I hear it's quite chic."

"The kids who join TALC go in but never come out."

"Uh-huh." Macklin finished the shake and dumped the paper cup amidst the pizza crust, Kleenex, and yogurt containers in the thin wicker basket beside the toilet.

"I'm joining them."

Macklin stared at her through the frosted glass. Her body was straight, and she was looking at him in an aloof, distant way.

"I want to find out exactly what's happening to those kids," she said.

"Yeah, that sounds great," he said. "But in practice it's pretty stupid. They are going to play around with your head. They're probably experts at it. You'll go in there as Ms. Gung-ho Journalist and come out as their publicity director."

"I know that, Brett," she said in a patronizing tone. "I'm taking precautions."

"There are other ways to tell the story. You don't need to go undercover."

"That's the way I want to do it."

The phone rang on the nightstand by the bed. Macklin glared at the phone as if that would shut it up. He glanced at Mordente, set his burger on the toilet tank, and reluctantly trudged out to the bedroom.

"Hello," he snapped.

"It's me," replied LAPD Sergeant Ronald Shaw, "the guy who should be home sleeping but is cleaning up your mess at the Chevron station instead."

The black homicide detective and Macklin had grown up together. It was Shaw, with Los Angeles mayor Jed Stocker's approval, who kept the LAPD from probing too deeply into Mr. Jury—the vigilante who had crushed a homicidal street gang, destroyed a ring of psychopathic pedophiles, and decimated a racist cult of deranged killers. The vigilante Brett Macklin had become.

Macklin turned and saw Mordente standing naked in front of the toilet, holding his hamburger with disdain over the toilet bowl.

"The attendant says the guys you toasted knew you," Shaw said.

She smiled at Macklin, dropped the burger in the toilet, and flushed it. Macklin grinned and turned his back to her.

"Yeah, they did."

"Shit, Mack, if the gangs know you're Mr. Jury, they're not going to rest until they've chopped you into little pieces," Shaw said. "You need protection."

Macklin glanced at his shoulder holster draped over a chair across the room. "Ronny, I've got all the protection I need."

"Give me a break, Mack. You aren't an invincible superhero. Tonight you were lucky. Tomorrow you may not be."

Macklin felt Mordente press her damp body against his back. She let her hands glide down his broad chest and over his flat stomach to his waist.

"It's time for you to give up this vigilante lunacy," Shaw said. "It's over. Move to another city or something and start again."

There were four dull pops as Mordente split open the buttons of his Levi's 501 jeans.

"Ronny, I've got to go." Her warm hands slipped under his bikini briefs. "Something just came up."

CHAPTER TWO

Wednesday, June 12, 8:30 a.m.

Their chests were heaving, their lungs clawing for air, as their bodies climbed the heights of their passion. Macklin felt the urgency in her hot breaths, in the trembling hands holding his neck.

Macklin sat at the bed's edge, his hands on Mordente's sides. She faced him, her eyes half-closed with pleasure, as she bobbed on his lap. The morning sun seeped through the shutters and sliced their sweaty bodies with beams of light.

He licked her lips with the tip of his tongue and brushed her erect nipples with his thumbs. She sucked in her stomach and involuntarily arched her back, offering her pleasure-hungry breasts to his hands.

"I can't hold out much longer," she gasped. "My hair will turn gray."

Macklin chuckled and kissed her, kneading her aching breasts. "Then I win."

She shook her head. "No way, damn it, you'll come first." She swallowed, trying to control her feverish breathing. "I can't afford to buy you dinner."

Her pelvic muscles squeezed tight around his penis. A bolt of pleasure shot up Macklin's spine. Her body rode him, pumping the pleasure in them both to an unbearable intensity. Macklin clutched her breasts and she saw his face become rigid.

"Having some problems?" she huffed, her face wrinkling as if she were about to sneeze.

Macklin shook his head and gritted his teeth, his upper lip quivering.

Their fingers dug into each other and a tremor rocked their bodies. Suddenly Mordente cried out, bouncing franticly and breathing in staccato bursts. Macklin stiffened, his face shaking, a low moan escaping from his lips. Their bodies shook with ecstasy, riding the orgasmic waves of pleasure.

Her movements gradually slowed and Macklin's body relaxed, a flush coloring his skin. She leaned forward and nuzzled her face against his neck.

"I think it's a draw," Macklin whispered, his eyes still closed.

Mordente laughed and hugged him tightly. She could feel his heart pounding against her. "So who buys dinner?"

The phone jangled.

"Shit." Macklin reached for it.

"It's me," Shaw said.

"Oh, for God's sake, Ronny, will you leave me alone?" Mordente laughed again and kissed his neck.

"I've got bad news, Mack."

Macklin kissed the top of her head. "Yeah, yeah, go on."

"Mort's been killed."

Every muscle in Macklin's body stiffened defensively. Mordente felt it and pulled back, staring into Macklin's cold eyes. For a second, she felt like she was the only person in the room.

"The Mexican police need you to come down and claim the body," Shaw said. "You're his only family."

"Tell me what happened." Macklin said in a monotone. Mordente slid off of him and sat on the bed, uncomfortably aware of her nakedness.

"I'm not sure. He was found in his hotel room with his neck broken," Shaw replied, pausing awkwardly for a moment before continuing to speak. "A cop named Ortiz will meet you at the airport. I'm sorry, Mack, I—"

"It's all right," Macklin interrupted. "I'll let you know if I find out anything."

"I'd go with you if I could."

"I know. I'll call you." Macklin slammed down the phone and pulled on his pants, which were lying in a clump beside the bed.

"What is it?" Mordente asked.

He picked up his chili-stained shirt and put it on. "Mort has been killed."

"Oh, Brett…" As she reached to touch him, he went to the closet.

He found a duffel bag and started shoving clothes into it. She watched him in silence and drew the sheets up over herself.

"Where are you going?"

"To Mexico. Someone's got to claim the body and someone has to find the killer." He dropped the duffel bag on the chair and strapped on his gun. "And make him pay."

He leaned over Mordente and gave her a light kiss on the lips. "Call my ex-wife. Tell her I can't take Cory to the movies tomorrow."

She nodded, put her hand behind his neck, and drew him to her lips again. He pulled back, looked into her moist eyes, and almost stayed.

He turned abruptly and walked out.

Noon

Brooke Macklin closed Isadora Van Rijn's portfolio and laid it gently on her desk. Van Rijn's paintings, depicted in the photographs in the portfolio, were among the most haunting works Brooke had ever seen. Yet, she could barely keep her attention on them. Van Rijn herself was the most haunting thing Brooke had ever seen. Brooke's eyes kept drifting over the edge of the portfolio and locking on the slim, black-haired woman who had just breezed in and, in a voice that had the intimacy of a whisper and the jarring effect of a shout, asked if she could show the owner her work.

Ordinarily, Brooke would have stifled an incredulous laugh and shown the obnoxious stranger to the door. Instead, with trancelike submission, Brooke had taken it.

Van Rijn was browsing through Brooke's gallery, studying the paintings with her soft amber eyes.

The pull, which Brooke couldn't quite define, didn't wane as time passed. It only grew stronger.

Van Rijn's coal black hair was styled in a blunt bob cut that accented her cheekbones and gave her eyes a sharp, mean quality. She wore a black wool jacket over a baggy V-neck T-shirt. Brooke noticed the large, dark nipples poking against the white fabric as it brushed over the smooth swell of Van Rijn's unrestrained breasts. Her jacket had narrow lapels and hung past her hips. The sleeves were bunched up over her elbows, and her hands were buried in the pockets of her black leather pants.

"Your work is captivating, unusual," Brooke began. *And so are you.* She had trouble summoning her voice. Van Rijn cocked her head towards Brooke and smiled, a sort of half-amused expression that gave Brooke a chill and a charge at the same time. "How come I've never heard of you?"

Van Rijn shrugged. "I've kept to myself."

"Isadora, I'll be honest with you. People don't just walk in here out of nowhere and expect me to give them a show," Brooke said.

"I understand," Van Rijn said, approaching Brooke's desk. "I appreciate your time and patience."

Van Rijn reached for her portfolio.

Brooke put her hand over Van Rijn's. "Wait," she said, self-consciously removing her tingling hand. "That isn't what I meant.

It's just that your work is so good, I can't believe you haven't been heard from before. I'd like to do a show with you."

The phone rang.

"Excuse me," Brooke said, swiveling her chair around so she faced the back of the store. "Cory? Could you get that?"

"Okay," replied a tiny voice in the back room.

"That's my daughter," Brooke explained, smiling. "She's teaching me and my staff how to use the computer I just bought."

"How old is she?" Van Rijn asked.

"Ten. And she's the only one who understands the damn thing."

Van Rijn laughed, a gentle sound that Brooke could feel tickling her sternum.

"Mom?" Cory walked out of the backroom and leaned against the doorjamb, crossing her arms under her chest. She had the stature of an adult and curious, intelligent eyes offset by a tiny pug nose crossed by a light sprinkle of freckles.

Brooke turned around and Cory continued: "It's Jessica. She wants to talk with you. She says it's important."

"Ask her if I can call her right back," Brooke said.

"Wait," Van Rijn interrupted. "I have to go now anyway. Is there another time I can see you?"

"How about this time tomorrow?"

"My days are complicated."

"Mom," Cory whined impatiently.

"Hold on," Brooke said sternly. She rolled her eyes at Isadora, as if to say, You know how it is ... "Why don't we get together for dinner? I'll have some contracts drawn up and we can get to know each other."

"All right."

Brooke scrawled something on the back of a business card and handed it to Van Rijn. "This is my home address. Why don't you come by Friday evening, about eight?"

Van Rijn nodded shyly, said, "Thank you," in a light, husky voice, turned, and walked out. Brooke sat in her chair for a long moment until Cory's insistent "Mahhhhm" jarred her from her inaction and freed her from the lingering scent of Van Rijn's subtle perfume.

Puerto Vallarta, Mexico, 3:00 p.m.

The palm trees were bent back against the hot, wet wind, their leaves fluttering. The frothing, bruised clouds crackled with quivering bolts of fire and crushed the morning's blue sky in resonant quakes. The afternoon storm seemed alive, a creature daring Brett Macklin to step out of his Cessna and face its wrath.

Macklin emerged from the plane braced for the worst, clutching his jacket collar tight around his neck. But, to his surprise, it was sweltering outside, the humid air hugging his face like a steaming towel. The contrast between the amiable air and the furious sky made Macklin uneasy. He wasn't quite sure how to react to it. He wasn't quite sure how to react to anything anymore.

Except violence. Ever since his father was set aflame by a street gang, death stalked Macklin. It was there, lurking in the shadows, wherever Macklin turned.

It was here, too, in this strange land. It had taken Mort as it had JD Macklin and Cheshire Davis... as it would someday take him.

Violence had become the only constant in Brett Macklin's life.

He pulled the hatch shut behind him and strode across the tarmac towards the small terminal building. Ahead and to his left, three passengers and two MexAir stewards filed up the mobile stairway into a 727.

The wind whipped Macklin's hair and the drizzle stung his face as he passed beside the plane. He imagined row after row of American tourists, wearing their ridiculous sombreros, waiting to be whisked back to their sedate world.

God, how he wished he could return to a time when violence to him was something that William Shatner did between commercials for Hamburger Helper and Fruit of the Loom. He had lived with the naive faith that he was safe from the savage dark side of humanity. He'd never thought about the fragile nature of his very existence; he'd wondered why nobody could make a frozen pizza that didn't taste like dry rot.

He glanced wistfully up into the cabin. A steward pulled a gun from inside his red blazer and motioned a stewardess down the aisle.

Macklin heard Fate giving him the Bronx cheer.

The other steward disappeared into the cockpit while a nervous stewardess began closing the plane's hatch. The familiar coldness washed over Brett Macklin and carried him forward. He dashed up the stairs like a flustered, rushed tourist.

"Wait, wait," he yelled, waving his duffel bag in the air, "don't go home without me!"

He came huffing into the plane and glanced apologetically to his right at the steward standing in the aisle. The man was breathing through his mouth, exposing his silver-capped incisors. Macklin couldn't see his gun, but he knew it was there by the expression on the stewardess's face. She stood behind the steward and looked like she might vomit.

"May I have your boarding pass, please?" asked the stewardess to Macklin's left. Behind her, the other steward stood in the cockpit doorway and, Macklin assumed, had a gun pointed at the woman's back.

"Sure," Macklin said, dropping his duffel bag and reaching into his jacket with his right hand.

In one quick motion, he yanked out his .357, shoved the stewardess aside, and shot the steward standing in the cockpit doorway. The slug burst open the steward's stomach, blasting out entrails and blood.

The seam between the passengers' world and Macklin's split open. They peeked in and recoiled in panic and revulsion. Some ped under their seats, others squirmed uncontrollably, a few just covered their ears and wailed. The cacophony of fear was lost in the deafening roar of gunfire.

Macklin spun into a crouch as the other steward's gun bucked. Macklin felt the searing trail of a bullet skimming over his head and pumped off two shots. The first bullet slammed into the steward's chest and spun him on his heels. The second bullet tore into his cheek, spraying the cabin with silver-capped teeth and bloody cartilage.

The blood-splashed stewardess in the aisle screamed, her horrified eyes locked on the convulsing, faceless corpse at her feet. Her scream became part of the echo of terror and gunfire that shuddered through the plane.

Macklin grimaced. Puerto Vallarta was just another battleground.

He stood up and twirled the gun around his finger so that he held it by the barrel. Avoiding the other stewardess's empty eyes, he bent over and snatched up his duffel bag. He let his gun arm hang limply against his side and calmly walked through the hatchway.

It was pouring rain. A lightning bolt flashed overhead and thunder rolled through the dark clouds. A half dozen soldiers scrambled out of the airport and aimed their rifles at him. One man, in a water-soaked khaki shirt and slacks, stood at the base of the stairway with his gun pointed at Macklin's gut. The man seemed oblivious to the drenching downpour.

Macklin slowly moved down the stairs and studied the man's face. It looked as though someone had run a steamroller over it a few times. The man's head was large, the skin puffy, the nose flat and wide.

The man regarded Macklin quizzically. "Are you Brett Macklin?"

Macklin nodded. Water streamed down his face, but he felt the death clinging to his skin, refusing to be washed away.

"We saw you leave your little plane and run into the jet." The man motioned to the .357 at Macklin's side. "You carry some interesting luggage, Mr. Macklin."

Macklin shrugged, offering the man the butt of his .357. "With this, I don't have to carry traveler's checks."

The man snorted, his lips twisted into a half-assed grin. He, too, had a couple of silver-capped teeth. Macklin hoped he'd never need a cavity filled in Mexico. The man holstered his gun and waved at the soldiers to lower their rifles.

"I'm Captain Jacob Ortiz of the Puerto Vallarta police." He took Macklin's .357, slipped it under his waistband, and led him towards the terminal. "I sincerely hope your stay will be short."

CHAPTER THREE

The downpour turned Puerto Vallarta's cobblestone streets into rivers of mud. The Chrysler sedan lumbered through like a barge.

Ortiz sat in the backseat beside Macklin, who squinted through the mud-smeared windshield at the thatched huts and chalky white buildings ahead.

"How long has the weather been like this?" Macklin asked. "It must be killing the tourist trade."

He felt the cold barrel of his .357 poke him in the side. Macklin glanced down at it in surprise and then up into Ortiz's impassive face.

"I guess you don't like small talk," Macklin said.

Ortiz nudged him with the gun. "Open your door."

Macklin pushed open the door. Muddy water splashed into the moving car. "If you wanted fresh air, you could have just asked me nicely."

"Jump out," Ortiz said.

Macklin sighed and looked glumly at the man. "You aren't Captain Ortiz."

"Brilliant deduction," the man said, "now jump."

Macklin hesitated. He knew it had been too good to be true. No one can step off a plane, kill a couple men two minutes later, and then expect to be politely escorted past customs into a waiting car without any hassles.

How could I be so goddamn stupid? I deserve to be tossed out of a moving car.

The man cocked the gun. "You either jump out or I blow you out."

"Shit," Macklin hissed, and tumbled out of the car. His body slammed into the cobblestone, knocking the breath out of him. He rolled off the embankment in a waterfall of sludge and dropped facefirst into a pool of mud.

He flopped over onto his back and lay there stunned for a moment, his eyes closed and face caked with mud. He could feel the coarse, dirty water riding over his skin like sandpaper. The raindrops felt like stones pummeling his body.

Welcome to Mexico, Macky boy.

He was starting to rise when a crushing weight on his neck forced him back down with a splash. His eyes flew open, and through the haze of rain, mud, and dizziness, he saw himself surrounded by trees. But no, they weren't trees, he realized—they were men. Macklin, barely able to breathe under the boot mashing his throat, to make out the dark human shape towering over him, grabbed the man's ankle and futilely tried to lift the boot off his throat. His lungs ached for air. Raindrops and dizziness clouded his vision. He couldn't get his arms to operate properly.

The men drew in close around him and simultaneously began kicking him. His body jerked between the men and he lost his grasp on the man's ankle. His arms fell like broken tree limbs to the ground. He was utterly helpless, a sack of flesh for them to stomp into bloody mush.

They're killing me…

His consciousness drowned in the inky blackness of agony.

Southern California
Wednesday, June 12 / Thursday, June 13

The old yellow school bus pulled off the eerily empty highway and bumped along through the black desert night on an unlit private

18

road. Despite the jostling, of the two dozen people aboard, only Jessica Mordente and one teenage boy were awake. He was in the back, puking up his dinner into a plastic Ralph's grocery bag.

All Mordente could see out of her window was darkness. Her head was tilted against the glass, her cheek pressed to the cold, smooth surface. She could feel the vibration of the engine trembling in her larynx.

She'd lost track of time. How many hours ago was she wandering down Hollywood Boulevard, a lost look on her face? How long since they had found her, embraced her, cajoled her into coming to their white house on stilts that faced the beach?

She ate their dinner, drank their wine, soaked up their reassuring words. She filed onto the bus with the rest of the lonely people they had found, the people who had never heard of the TALC before but were ready to join it if it would just end their desperation.

How long until they arrived at the Talcon Colony? Hours? Days? No, she knew it couldn't be days. She knew where it was. It was in the desert somewhere...right? Mordente reminded herself that she was different from the others on the bus. She wasn't a lonely waif. She was a reporter.

Mordente tried to feel the immensity of the *Los Angeles Times*, the power of journalistic responsibility, lifting her up. It didn't work. The newsprint, the presses, and the green, luminescent letters on her VDT screen seemed far away.

Her eyes stung with fatigue, her butt ached from sitting so long, and her head felt heavy; they all were signals for her to let her body switch off. She knew she should be sleeping, but something kept her awake—curiosity, perhaps, and the desire not to give in to sleep as the others had. After all, she reminded herself again, she was different.

The bus turned, the motion swaying her body and lifting her cheek away from the glass. The gray wall of the Talcon Colony was revealed in the arc of the bus's headlights.

The driver honked twice. A simple iron gate, the only break in a sandblasted stone wall, swung open, and it became daylight in the desert. Dozens of hidden floodlights burst on atop the ten-foot stone wall and from their mountings in surrounding rocks and foliage.

An austere, pastel-colored hacienda with a faded, red-tile roof seemed to rise out of the night as the bus turned into the compound. Two unimaginative, barrack-style wings jutted from the main house. Mordente guessed they were built later, judging by the incongruence they created when matched with the hacienda.

The bus stopped with a lurch that made everyone on board jerk forward and wake up. Gears screeched, the engine coughed to death, and the doors folded back, letting the chilly desert suck the warmth out of the bus.

Mike, one of the TALC guys who had befriended Mordente on Hollywood Boulevard, popped into the aisle from one of the front seats. He looked about twenty-five and exuded so much energy, it looked to Mordente like a spotlight was on him. He was the sort of clean-cut type you find all over Provo, Utah, and wore a beige button-down oxford and a maroon sweater. His hands were half-buried in the pockets of his faded blue jeans, so his arms were crooked at the elbows, giving his upper body a sheepish, golly-gee-whiz hunch. His rubber-tipped, blue canvas tennis shoes added to the impression.

"Here we are, my new friends," he said, his smile unwavering. "You're with family now."

The Mike clones, who also worked for TALC, were sprinkled throughout the bus and clapped enthusiastically, stoking applause in their new charges.

"Total awareness and a new life"—he paused for effect—"begin now."

The brilliant white light that bathed the compound spilled through the bus doorway, casting a glow that reminded Mordente of the gaping entrance to the mother ship in *Close Encounters of the Third Kind*. Mike swept his right arm towards the door, bidding them all to step through the gateway to a better way of life. Mordente expected to hear a chorus of angels at any moment.

She hid her cynicism behind a mask of blank acceptance and shuffled out of the bus obediently with the others. She shielded her face with her arm against the painful glare from the klieg lights mounted on the sprawling hacienda's rooftop. If she squinted, she could make out two figures standing on the veranda across from the bus.

One wore a turban and sunglasses, apparently mistaking the klieg lights for the scorching desert sun. He was a few yards away but his body odor seeped out of his khaki shirt, which was unbuttoned to his belly. Mordente figured his shirt was gaping open because he was afraid he'd snag all that chest hair in the buttons. Or suffocate in his own BO.

The man beside him, Mordente assumed, had no nasal passages. He was also a lot more relaxed, casually dressed in a gray sweatshirt and faded blue jeans. Mordente squinted at Mr. Arab and Mr. Relaxed and wondered when the TALC leader, Fraser Nebbins, would make his grand appearance.

"Howdy," Mr. Relaxed said, plunging his hands into his pockets and shuffling forward to the veranda steps. "I'm Fraser Nebbins."

Mordente was caught completely off guard. Where was the full-size, glib prototype from which Mike and his legion of clones were born? Where was the smooth talker armored in three-piece Yves Saint Laurent who danced like John Travolta around press inquires? Where was the pomp, the show, the bullshit?

Nebbins stood in front of the line of street urchins like a general facing his troops. "I welcome you, my brothers and sisters, into our family." A smile rich in family warmth bloomed on his face. "Here you will have the peace and freedom to explore your inner selves and experience total awareness." He walked down the line of people, smiling at each of them, shaking hands, stroking hair. "These walls, and the brothers and sisters carrying firearms, aren't here to keep you in. They are here to keep the corruption and disease that's out there ... out there."

Meek chuckles rippled through the line and Mordente felt her pulse quicken anxiously as Nebbins approached her.

"It isn't long before you forget life out there completely." He reached out his hand to Mordente's cheek and lightly stroked it. "Sleep well, everyone. Tomorrow you begin new lives."

Mordente lowered her head shyly and followed the others towards the rear of the hacienda. Nebbins crossed his arms under his chest, his eyes admiring the smooth curves of Mordente's slim body as she disappeared around the building's edge.

Achmed Sabib stepped quietly to Nebbins' side.

"She's stunning," Nebbins muttered.

Sabib absently scratched the hair on his chest. "Yes, she'll fetch us a good price."

Nebbins shared a grin with his friend. "Let's give her a test drive ourselves first, eh?"

They clapped their arms around each other and laughed quietly as they walked back into the hacienda, the floodlights clicking off behind them and submerging the colony in blackness once again.

Jessica Mordente knew what was happening to her. They were breaking her. And she didn't know how much longer she could hold on to her sanity.

The cell was pitch-black. The only light she saw was when she closed her eyes. Then it was the Fourth of July. The fireworks were dazzling, almost hypnotic, and she was afraid of it. When she opened her eyes, the colorful explosions of brilliant brightness disappeared. So she kept her eyes open and hungered for the light.

When she first entered the barracks (how long ago was that?), three men grabbed her and hit her until she was nearly unconscious. She was aware of them stripping off her clothes and jamming a needle in her arm.

Then everything was warm and she couldn't move. Her thoughts became disjointed, and everything she saw looked like reflections in a carnival Fun House mirror. They carried her down a cramped, dimly lit corridor that was hot with the smell of human sweat. They tossed her into a concrete cell. A single lightbulb entwined in cobwebs dangled from the ceiling. It had been on then. There was no window, no bed, no toilet. Just a hole in the center of the room.

The light went out before her head cleared. She crawled into a corner and curled up, shivering, staring into the blackness. She heard the ringing. It began softly at first and then became louder. It wouldn't go away. It just droned on and on, incessantly, drilling into her skull. She was sure that once it got inside, even if they turned off the sound, it would never go away.

She wasn't claustrophobic before, but now she could feel the unseen walls closing in on her in the darkness, pushing out the air, smothering her. Her breathing became deep and hungry, her lungs aching for air.

She closed her eyes against the fear and the brilliant whiteness returned, bathing her in an intense, soothing glow. A tingling sensation rode up her legs and traveled everywhere, across her chest, under her arms, over her lips. It felt like...

Her quivering hands rose to her face and she felt the hard insect bodies scurrying across her skin, into her hair, down her neck. She screamed hysterically and bounced herself madly off the cell walls until she collapsed, quivering, onto the floor and let the white light in her head claim her.

CHAPTER FOUR

Puerto Vallarta, Mexico
Thursday, June 13, 11:32 a.m.

"You should have listened to Karl Malden, Harv," Ivy Goldblatt said as they shuffled down the cobblestone road, adjusting her tube top every few steps. "We wouldn't be in this mess if we had American Express."

She punctuated her sentences by poking her husband in the shoulder with her index finger. It didn't bother him. Thirteen years of marriage to her had left tiny calluses all over his body. Other people, though, left conversations with Ivy looking like they'd been pistol-whipped.

"Shut up, Ivy." Harv shuffled along the embankment, his body hunched under the oppressive midmorning heat. "It doesn't make a goddamn difference what kind of checks we had. The goddamn bandito didn't ask me what was in the wallet before he lifted it, Ivy."

"Listen, mouth, where are you going to get a refund on Wanderin' Joe's traveler's checks here? Huh?"

"Yeah, and if you hadn't handed every goddamn peso we had to every goddamn street hoodlum selling phony jewelry, we could hail a fucking taxi."

His sunburned face felt like someone had used it for a pin cushion. The six coats of medicated Noxzema he had applied to his face that morning hadn't done a damn thing except make him smell funny. He was frustrated, uncomfortable, and tired and had to piss so bad he was afraid if he stopped moving his bladder would burst.

Some vacation.

"We should have taken the Love Boat cruise, Harv." Ivy poked him in the ribs and pulled up her tube top. "This is all your fault."

"That's it." Harv stopped, turned his back to the road, and started unbuckling his pants. "I'm gonna water the plants."

He unzipped his fly and fumbled with the flap in his underwear.

"Harv!" Ivy shrieked. "You can't do that. We're in a foreign country."

"Just watch the goddamn road or I'll whiz on you."

Harv sighed contentedly as he relieved himself off the edge of the embankment. He admired the nice, fine stream of urine spraying into the foliage and remembered those great high school piss contests. They used to see who could stand farthest from the toilet and still piss into it.

He always won. He was the undisputed Pissmaster.

Harv peered into the brush to see what he was drilling into. He was probably pounding some boulder into sand with his manly spray. But then he saw that it wasn't a rock he was hitting. It was a body.

"Holy shit." Harv's eyebrows climbed up his forehead. He let go of himself and stood very still, pissing into his shoe.

1:00 p.m.
The two attendants slid the stretcher carrying a bloodied, unconscious Brett Macklin into the white, '71 Cadillac ambulance and slammed the door shut.

Captain Jacob Ortiz combed his fingers through his shoulder-length brown hair and watched the ambulance shriek away down the street towards the hospital.

This Brett Macklin was one unlucky guy. And so, it seemed, were his friends—Ortiz had reread the autopsy report on Mort Suderson on his way over.

Although he couldn't prove it yet, Ortiz knew Macklin had thwarted the hijacking. All right, so the police hadn't been able to form a composite drawing from all the disparate descriptions they got from the passengers. But Macklin's plane had just landed and he would have been walking to the terminal at the time of the hijacking.

By the time Ortiz had showed up at the airport, the place was in pandemonium and Macklin was already gone. The man pretending to be Ortiz disappeared with Macklin before airport security realized they had been tricked.

Ortiz believed there was no connection between the hijacking and Macklin's abduction by the imposter. An unfortunate coincidence. In a way, he was glad Macklin was there. Macklin handled himself well. Too well. Christ, it was like Macklin was just swatting flies. Clearly, this was no ordinary man. And someone, a real pro, was going to a lot of trouble, risk, and expense to make life miserable for him.

But to what end? Why was Macklin still alive?

Ortiz loosened his red leather tie and opened his black-checked shirt at the collar. Ivy Goldblatt poked him in the chest, intruding into his thoughts, and once again he was listening to her drone.

"Okay, Mrs. Goldblatt," he interrupted. "I'll see if I can contact this guy, ah"—he looked at his notepad—"Karl Malden, for you about your traveler's checks."

"No, no," she said, stabbing him twice with her finger, "It's Wandering Joe. He's the one."

"All right, Wandering Joe, then." Ortiz put up his hands defensively to ward off any more blows. "I assure you, we won't leave you to roam the streets penniless."

"Thank you. You're very understanding considering we come from two different cultures," she said.

"We don't. I'm on loan from the LAPD," Ortiz said. "I'm the law enforcement version of an exchange student."

"You don't dress like a police officer," Ivy said with challenging eyes.

"I don't have to." Ortiz grinned. "They expect American cops to be different."

"But you're Mexican, aren't you?" Harv asked, studying his face.

"A Judeo-Mex-American." Ortiz grinned. He loved saying that to people.

Ivy Goldblatt paled. "You're Jewish?"

Ortiz nodded.

"Captain Ortiz?" an officer yelled behind him.

"Excuse me," Ortiz said to the Goldblatts and went to the car. "What is it, Mendoza?" he asked the officer in Spanish.

"They've located Sergeant Shaw," Mendoza replied. "They've got him on the phone at the station."

"Tell them to keep him on the line," Ortiz said. "I'm on my way."

❧   ❧   ❧

Achmed Sabib, his arms folded under his chest, stared into Jessica Mordente's empty eyes. She stood, naked, just an inch away from him, her gaze trained on some distant dimension outside of Nebbins' wood-paneled study.

"She's gone," Sabib marveled, waving his hand in front of her expressionless face. She had been washed, her skin moisturized, her hair shampooed, and her teeth brushed.

"Oh, she's still here." Nebbins petted her shiny, fluffy hair and looked at Sabib over her tan shoulder. "Just enough of her, anyway, to pleasure us and our buyers. Think of her as a warm, giving robot."

Sabib slapped his palm between her legs. Mordente didn't react. "I could stuff a hot poker in her and she'd never notice."

Nebbins' lips stretched into a malefic grin. "That's the idea, isn't it?"

"Nobody wants an empty bag of flesh, Nebbins."

"Don't worry, Achmed." Nebbins walked around Mordente and clapped Sabib reassuringly on the shoulder. "She's still a fetus."

Nebbins stroked her cheek with the back of his hand. "My perfect program of deprivation, malnutrition, isolation, and drugs will make her unusually receptive to suggestion and manipulation without damaging her capacity for hard labor or sexual functioning." He strode to an overstuffed leather chair across the room and sat down, draping a leg over one of the armrests. "That's what makes my product the Mercedes of the mass-market slave trade."

"How are the others coming?"

"Three proved unmalleable and had to be killed," Nebbins said. "The others are developing nicely. We may be slightly over-stocked with men, though."

"So we trim our inventory if necessary." Sabib pinched Mordente's lips.

Nebbins shrugged. "Some of them I'll allocate as specimens for research and development. I hate to be wasteful. This one, though, looks like she'll reap us many rewards."

Sabib studied her face and passionlessly fondled her breasts, examining them for workmanship. "So when can I begin reaping?"

"Patience, Achmed, patience." Nebbins grinned. "You can christen her on Sunday."

✣ ✣ ✣

Brett Macklin tumbled weightlessly through time and space, through the wispy clouds of memories real and memories imagined. The rhythmic, electronic bleeps of his electrocardiograph echoed from the furthest edges of his consciousness and scored his tormenting descent ...

... he was in Mayor Jed Stocker's office. Shaw was there, too.

The mayor sat at his desk. "I told you about the problem in Chinatown because I want Mr. Jury to take care of it."

"Fuck off, Stocker," Macklin said. "I'm not doing anything for you."

"You will. You're still angry. You want to keep fighting."

Macklin glanced at Shaw. The black detective's eyes reflected an eerie, sad anger. Macklin turned, strode to the office door, and flung it open.

He was in a MexAir plane. Everything looked murky, thick, as if submerged in water. He jerked his head over his shoulder and looked through the doorway. Stocker's office was gone. All he saw was the Puerto Vallarta airport terminal behind him.

"May I have your boarding pass, please?" the stewardess beside him asked. She spoke like a record played far too slow. Macklin looked down the long, endless aisle. Brooke and Cory sat in every seat. They sat, he knew, in judgment. A ghastly image of himself stood in the aisle laughing, his pasty lips twisted in unrestrained disgust around swollen, bleeding gums and silver-capped teeth.

"May I have your boarding pass, please?" the stewardess repeated in that heavy half speed of dreams.

Macklin grinned cockily at his alter image and, in that same, drowsy slowness, said, "Sure."

He pulled out his .357, spun on his heel, and fired at the silver-toothed Macklin.

The stewardess droned endlessly over the painful reverbera-
tions of the gunshot. "May I have your boarding pass, please?"

Brooke and Cory joined the uninjured, silver-toothed image
in sickly, malicious laughter. Macklin, confused, looked down at
his chest. He was bleeding, gallons and gallons of blood, unreal,
unthinkable, unbelievable streams of blood. The thick, frothing
waves of red bubbled out of his body, splashed on the floor, and
raged down the aisle.

"Who are you?" Brooke, Cory, and the silver-toothed Macklin
screeched, their voices like chalk skidding across a blackboard.
Macklin's blood lapped at their ankles. "Who are you?"

Macklin lifted his head from his wound and said, "The jury."

He dropped to his knees, the life spilling out of him.

"Who are you?" they wailed.

"The jury," Macklin yelled and fell forward. He grabbed at the
air, uselessly reaching for something to stop his fall. He splashed
face-first into a hot, bottomless pool of his own blood. He opened
his mouth to cry for help. Blood rushed up his nostrils and filled
his lungs, and he knew he was dead.

CHAPTER FIVE

Puerto Vallarta
Friday, June 14, 6:12 p.m.

The way Brett Macklin was feeling, he almost wished he actually was dead. He could feel the two hemispheres of his brain pulsing with a dull, swollen ache. His eyeballs floated in stinging oil, and the muscles in his body had been replaced with cement. So he just laid motionless in his bed, staring up at Jesus crucified on the wall above the iron headboard.

Macklin made no effort to contact anyone when he awoke, nor did he try to look at his watch, which wasn't on his wrist anyway. He was still getting used to the idea that he was alive, when the door to his room cracked opened and Captain Jacob Ortiz edged in.

"You're awake," Ortiz said, closing the door and disappearing again. The captain's sudden appearance prompted Macklin to focus his attention on his situation. Before he could do much thinking, the door opened again and Ortiz came in, accompanied by a doctor.

"How are you feeling?" Ortiz asked.

"I'll know in a minute," Macklin replied hoarsely as the doctor pulled back the bedsheets, exposing Macklin's wounds to them all.

His chest was bruised and his midsection was wrapped tightly in bandages. Bruises blotched the length of his legs.

"I'm better than I expected," Macklin said, raising his hands to his face, lightly brushing the swollen skin, and then over his head, which was covered with bandages.

The doctor smiled, listened to Macklin's heart with a stethoscope, said something to Ortiz in Spanish, and then left the two men alone.

"So?" Macklin asked. "What did he say?"

"He says you're lucky to be alive." Ortiz sat on the edge of Macklin's bed.

"How long have I been here?"

"Couple days," Ortiz replied. "You don't have any serious injuries, a few broken ribs and a lot of bruising, but the concussion and the trauma put you in a coma."

Macklin explored the inside of his mouth with his tongue. "What about my teeth? You didn't have to do anything to my teeth, did you?"

"Nope."

Macklin grinned. "Thank God. So who are you?"

Ortiz chuckled. "Aren't I the one who is supposed to ask the questions?"

"Yeah, but you won't get any answers unless I know who you are."

"I'm Captain Jacob Ortiz, Puerto Vallarta police."

"Great," Macklin said. "The last guy who told me that tossed me out of a moving car."

"That's what puzzles me, Mr. Macklin," Ortiz said. "Why would someone want to do that to you?"

Macklin would have shrugged if it wouldn't hurt like hell to do it. He just stared blankly at Ortiz instead.

"Why would someone want to kill your friend?" Ortiz continued. "Why would someone beat you and leave you to be pissed on?"

"Pissed on?"

"At first I thought you were one very unlucky man," Ortiz said. "But I was wrong, very wrong."

"What's this about being pissed on?"

"You're lucky I'm actually an LA cop, you're lucky to have a friend like Sergeant Shaw to pull strings for you, and you're lucky to be alive."

Macklin sat up slowly, gritting his teeth against the pain that squeezed his entire body with excruciating pressure.

"Someone pissed on me?"

Ortiz nodded. "Be glad. Otherwise, we might not have found you until there was nearly nothing left to find."

"I'm going to kill the motherfuckers who did this to me." Macklin turned his head to the bedside table. He saw the jug of water and the empty glass beside it. While Macklin was still deciding whether he wanted to try and get the water for himself, Ortiz stood up and poured Macklin a glass, holding it to Macklin's lips.

Macklin jerked his head away and took the glass from Ortiz's hand, spilling some of the water on himself in the process.

"Thanks," Macklin said, taking a sip.

"You're welcome." Ortiz sighed and sat down on the bed again.

"Tell me about Mort." Macklin swallowed all the water, leaned his head back against the wall, and closed his eyes.

"Suderson was found in his hotel room by a maid," Ortiz said. "We think a woman broke his neck while he was performing oral sex on her."

Macklin's eyes flew open. "What?"

"His face was soaked with vaginal discharge and there's evidence that extreme pressure was applied to either side of his head, " Ortiz said. "The position of his body when we found him clearly shows that he was on his knees at the time of his death. In addition, the traces of vaginal fluid we've found on the bedsheets and the carpet support the scenario."

Ortiz looked away so Macklin couldn't see the smile he could no longer hold back. "We don't think he was an accidental victim of unrestrained, overly enthusiastic orgasmic response. It was murder."

"A grotesquely appropriate way to kill him," Macklin observed. "Too appropriate."

Ortiz looked back at Macklin. "Who killed him?"

"You tell me," Macklin said. "I came down here to identify the body."

"And you almost became a corpse yourself." Ortiz stood up and paced. "C'mon, Mr. Macklin, let's not play games."

"Ortiz, I don't know anything. I'm more confused than you are."

Ortiz stopped and stared at Macklin as if the truth would suddenly appear in print on Macklin's forehead. "No, you aren't."

Macklin toyed with saying "yes, I am," but thought better of it. There was nothing to be gained by needling the man and everything to lose. He knew Ortiz could make life even less pleasant than it was now. *I did kill two men,* he thought, *and they could hold me forever on that. Or they could disclose to the press that I was the guy who did it.*

"What about the woman. Do you have any leads on her?" Macklin asked.

"A description from people at the pool where Suderson met her," Ortiz said. "Unfortunately, it's difficult to identify someone only from descriptions of her buttocks and breasts. Suderson, however, they all remembered."

Macklin couldn't help grinning. Mort never was very subtle, even in death.

"We've got passenger lists for all the outgoing flights since Suderson's murder, including the flight you ... ah ... disrupted," Ortiz said. "You're going to go through them and see if any name jogs your memory."

"Okay, go get them."

Ortiz was surprised. He thought Macklin would claim to be too weak, or in too much pain, to be helpful. Ortiz walked to the door, opened it a crack, and stuck his head into the corridor.

"Mendoza," he yelled, "bring me the lists."

Ortiz returned to Macklin's bed holding a sheaf of computer printouts and laid them on Macklin's lap. Macklin lifted the scroll and began scanning the names.

Alberts, Penelope... Ames, Trisha... Arness, Frances. Banks, Helen...

"This whole thing makes no sense at all to me," Ortiz said. "What did these unknown assailants gain by abducting you?"

... Bender, Karen ... Biagas, Loraine ... Boucher, Laura ... Byrd, Betty ... Cabrera, Lucy ...

"They went to a lot of trouble and risk to do it, too," Ortiz continued. "But to what end?"

Carlson, Elisa ... Copeland, Dorothy ... Curran, Janice ... .

"They didn't take your wallet or your watch," Ortiz said, "and they didn't beat you badly enough to kill you. They left you where you could presumably be found. I mean, they could easily have killed you if that's what they wanted."

Davenport, Katie ... Davidson, Burl ... Davis, Cheshire ...

Cheshire Davis.

Macklin felt a shiver course his spine. The killer, whoever she was, had a cruel, acidic sense of humor. Cheshire had been Macklin's lover. A gang of psychopathic pedophiles had tried to kill him by planting a bomb in his car. They'd killed Cheshire instead.

The killer chose the name knowing I'd see it, Macklin thought. The killer is having fun with me. The killer is going to pay.

"Why didn't the kidnappers kill you?" Ortiz continued. "All they succeeded in doing was putting you in the hospital for a few days."

Macklin looked up from the printout.

"What did you say?"

"I said, what were the guys after? All they managed to do was put you in bed for a while."

And keep me out of Los Angeles, away from … away from Brooke, from Cory, from—

"Get me a phone," Macklin snapped.

"What?" Ortiz was startled.

"Get me a phone, damn it." Macklin tossed the printout at him. "I want to call my family."

"Cory is at a slumber party for the weekend," Brooke told Macklin over the phone. She was doing a poor job of hiding her exasperation. Mack had become so difficult lately. She could barely hear his barrage of questions because of static and the echo of her own voice on the line.

"With who?" he demanded.

"Her friends, Mack. Cory and a bunch of her friends are with the Hendersons at their cabin up at Big Bear Lake. Is that okay with you?"

"What are you doing?"

"None of your damn business, Mack," Brooke said, wincing as echoes of her words blared into her ear. "What the hell is the matter with you?"

"Nothing, Brooke, nothing at all," Macklin replied somberly. "I just wanted to know both of you were all right."

She stayed quiet for a moment, smiled at her dinner guest, and waited for the echoes to clear the line.

"We're all right, okay? Give the interrogation routine a rest."

"Be careful, Brooke, and keep a close eye on Cory," Macklin said. "You could be in some danger."

Oh God, she thought, *not this paranoid crap again.* Last time she'd let him nag her into leaving town. "No one's out to get us, Mack," she said.

"Don't be so sure," Macklin replied. "Mort's death wasn't an accident."

Brooke paused to consider her reply. Mort was probably killed by some tramp's enraged husband. Unfortunately, Brett had faced two other deaths in the last year or so, and a smart-ass reply wouldn't do much good. After all, anybody in his shoes would start to get a little unhinged.

"I'm sorry about Mort, I really am," Brooke said carefully. "But I haven't seen him in years and I never had much connection with the guy anyway. I doubt whoever wanted to hurt him would care about Cory and me."

"Brooke—"

"Look, Mack, I have to go," Brooke interrupted. "I have guests. Give Cory a call when she gets back Sunday night, okay?"

"Take care, Brooke."

"I will. Good-bye." Brooke hung up the phone and exhaled, sagging on her bar stool at the kitchen counter.

Brooke carried her empty glass to the table, where the dirty dinner plates sat unattended, and poured herself some more of the chilled wine, which was now lukewarm.

"That was my ex-husband, Brett." She filled her glass. "His father was murdered not long ago, and ever since then he's been behaving strangely."

She walked to the couch and cleared a space for herself among the dozens of hand-knit pillows.

"I just don't know how to deal with him anymore."

"Tell me about him." Isadora Van Rijn smiled warmly and put her arm around Brooke. "Maybe I can help."

CHAPTER SIX

"Where's the cat?" Laura asked, pushing open the cabin's screen door and stepping out onto the porch. She clasped her pink bathrobe tight around her neck against the cold night air and looked down at the hand-made clay cat dish, decorated with Garfield cartoons and glazed yellow. "She hasn't even touched her Tender Vittles. Rusty, have you seen the cat?"

"No," Rusty replied from inside the cabin, "and if I do I'm gonna clean the toilet bowl with it. Why don't you come back in here and watch Johnny Carson with me?"

She let the screen door slam behind her and stared into the wall of trees where the light cast from the porch melted into darkness. Crickets hummed and a gentle breeze wafted across the lake and ruffled through the tall trees.

"I'm going to go look for the cat."

"Lore-ahhhh," he drawled, "you don't want to be out there looking for the cat."

"Yes, I do." She stomped off the porch into the trees, her yellow thongs slapping against her heels with every step.

"For Christ's sake, Laura, have you forgotten about the escaped convict?" Rusty wailed. "Laura, did you hear me? Laura?"

She didn't hear him. She had already stormed angrily into the thicket, just glad she was going to be away from Rusty's Schlitz-y breath and clammy hands when Loni Anderson came on the Carson show. Loni and her trampy hair and cow teats always made him horny.

But her irritation soon cooled in the night air and she ran out of steam, stopping dead in her tracks. She stood still. The night closed in around her. She became aware of the crushing silence and the impenetrable darkness and realized she care didn't if Cuddles ate his Vittles or not.

She heard a crunch, the sound of leaves being crushed underfoot. Her head jerked instinctively towards the sound. It was behind her.

"Cuddles?" she ventured. Another crunch, then another. Something was moving towards her. She stayed planted to the ground, as immobile as the trees around her. "Cuddles?"

Suddenly there was a loud shriek. She stumbled backwards, startled, as a half dozen loons burst out of the brush screaming, wings fluttering, and flew off in every direction. She clutched her robe at the chest and felt her heart thumping excitedly. *Loons.* She sighed gratefully. *Just some loony loons.*

She was still looking at the trees where the birds took flight when she saw a familiar flash of blue terry cloth.

"Rusty, what the hell were—," she began, but then stopped. Her husband emerged from the trees, moving slowly towards her, his arms flush against his sides, his eyes staring past her, his jaw hanging open.

Then he stopped, just a few feet away from her, his lower lip twitching.

"Rusty, what's the matter with you?" she said, planting her hands firmly on her sides. "Why are you acting like a zombie or something?"

A sound, the beginnings of a word, growled in his throat, and then he tipped forward onto the ground. And she saw the ax buried deep in his back.

Laura's terrified scream melded with the killer's banshee cry of manic glee as he came running out of the trees like a pole vaulter, holding a pitchfork. Cuddles the cat was speared on the end.

She back-stepped into a run, clamoring wildly into the trees, yelling for help.

"Cuddles wants to seeee you," he cried after her, his pea coat flaring out like wings as he ran.

Laura scrambled through the brush, jerking her head around to see him gaining on her, his face alight with a wild, toothy grin. She screamed, stumbled, and went flailing into a tangle of bushes.

He loomed over her and held the pitchfork poised over her head. The cat's blood streaked down the three muddy prongs and dripped onto her pale, anxious face.

"Here," he hissed, "give Cuddles a kissy-poo."

The man wrinkled his face with disgust and brought all his weight down against the pitchfork...and a dozen fifth-grade girls squealed with gleeful terror and cowered in their sleeping bags, the glow from the TV set the only light in the Hendersons' dark living room.

"Their parents are going to kill me," Nina Henderson groaned in the kitchen, plucking the ten candles from her daughter Becky's birthday cake. "How could you let Becky talk you into renting *Bloodbath Daycamp for Girls?*"

Jake Henderson grinned at her from across the table, where he was dropping the paper plates and party favors into a Glad trash bag. "So what? It's her birthday—let her have a little fun."

"*Bloodbath Daycamp for Girls,*" she repeated to herself as she put the cake in the refrigerator. Her husband set down his bag and tiptoed to the doorway and peeked into the living room.

The girls were all huddled around the set, their eyes wide, the light from the TV flickering like a campfire. His daughter Becky watched the movie while braiding Cory Macklin's long blond hair.

Nina Henderson flicked off the kitchen lights and pressed herself against her husband's back, wrapping her arms around his waist and patting his stomach.

"C'mon, Jake," she whispered into his ear, "let's leave them alone and go upstairs."

The phone in the kitchen rang shrilly, startling them both.

"Ignore it," she mumbled.

Jake shrugged apologetically, untangled himself from Nina, and went to the phone. "Hello?"

"Jake, this is Brett Macklin."

"Hey, how'ya doing?" Jake said. "I haven't heard from you in ages."

Who is it? Nina mouthed.

Brett Macklin, he mouthed in return.

Nina shot a confused look at Jake and then peered into the living room at Cory, who was frozen with the rest of the girls, their attention captured by something suspenseful on the screen.

"Want me to get Cory for you?" Jake said.

"No," Macklin said quickly, "that's all right. I just wanted to check in and see if everything is okay."

Jake scratched his forehead. "Ah, yeah, everything's fine, Brett. Why?"

"Just wondering," Macklin said. "Do me a favor, keep your eye on Cory, okay?"

Jake glanced at Nina, who was spying on the girls. "We've got our eye on her right now."

"Make sure she gets home all right," Macklin said, "and don't leave her alone."

"Sure," Jake said.

"Thanks." Macklin hung up.

Jake stared at the receiver. "He's nutso."

Brooke talked incessantly. It was the wine. It was the quiet of the apartment. It was the insistence of Isadora Van Rijn's eyes looking into her own.

"Your work is scary but it draws you in anyway," Brooke said, uncomfortably aware of the warmth of Isadora's arm around her. "That one with the faceless, naked woman sitting on top of the man, pinning his neck between her knees. It's as if she's strangling him with her femininity. It's unsettling as hell."

Isadora smiled and remained quiet, leaving Brooke to flounder in the pressuring silence.

"There's poetry to your violence, though." Brooke was trying to fill the room with words and force out the tension. She knew she was saying things thoughtlessly and wondered, for a second, if she sounded foolish. But the silence was more threatening. Her body was buzzing in a scary, thrilling way, and she wasn't sure if she liked it or not. "Your images are fraught with sexuality, death, and emotion. Where do you get them from?"

Isadora's other hand dropped gently onto Brooke's thigh. It choked the words rising in Brooke's throat, and she felt a hot flush ride over her. She met Isadora's gaze directly and gave in to what she knew she had been feeling all night. Isadora let her hand gently stroke the soft skin of Brooke's thigh and leaned slowly towards her.

Brooke knew she wouldn't stop her. She had been resisting these feelings for hours. *Go ahead,* Brooke thought, staring into Isadora's dark eyes. *I don't know what's going to happen, but I want to find out.*

She couldn't say these things to Isadora—she simply challenged her with her gaze. Isadora pressed her face close to Brooke's throat and let her hand slide up Brooke's flank.

Brooke felt Isadora's breath on her skin, warming it, making it tingle. She enjoyed a deliciously precarious feeling of hanging over a precipice, awaiting the inevitable fall into something wonderful.

Isadora sat up straight and took Brooke's wrists roughly in her hands. "Do you want the kiss?"

Brooke heard herself breathe out, "Yes."

"Then what I do for you, you will do for me."

Isadora pushed her down onto the pillows and kissed her deeply on the mouth. Brooke moved past thinking and let herself be led wherever Isadora was taking her. Isadora kissed her again, softer, with a tenderness Brooke didn't think was possible. Their lips barely touched, just enough to spark sensation. It made Brooke hungry for more. Her pelvis ground against Isadora and her breasts swelled.

The kissing stopped. Brooke heard herself panting. *Don't stop now…* She needed more from Isadora, wanted more. Then Brooke felt Isadora's moist tongue on her soft, sensitive neck. Isadora was drawing tiny circles on Brooke's neck with her tongue, barely touching the skin. It was an incredible feeling. Every time Isadora's tongue touched her skin, Brooke felt a pleasurable pulse between her legs. Brooke's chest rose and fell with increasing urgency. Isadora sensed Brooke's rising passion. She smoothed her hand over the delicate softness of Brooke's full, swelling breast. Brooke dug her nails into the couch cushions, stunned by the intensity of the pleasure she felt from Isadora's touch.

Isadora began to unbutton Brooke's blouse. Brooke longed for Isadora's gentle caress on her flushed, increasingly sensitive skin. She gasped when she felt Isadora's tongue brush the back of her neck. Her tongue glided over Brooke's neck, slid down the strong line of her sternum, and stopped at the rise of her quivering breasts. Brooke moaned weakly, her breasts aching for the withheld touch, and stared helplessly into Isadora's amber eyes. *Please…*

Isadora sat up, straddling Brooke's waist, and peeled open Brooke's blouse to reveal her breasts, starkly pale against the dark tan of the rest of her skin. Brooke had never felt so vulnerable or so lustful. It was wonderfully frightening.

Brooke could see Isadora's nipples pressing against her fuzzy white angora sweater and had to touch them. With trembling fingers, Brooke tentatively reached for Isadora's breasts, brushing the hard nipples and kneading the warm flesh. She could feel Isadora's heartbeat quickening.

Giving Isadora pleasure, arousing this perfect creature, heightened Brooke's excitement. She felt a giddy, transcendent sense of physical euphoria. She wanted Isadora to feel the desire she felt, to crave that ultimate release as badly as she did.

Isadora closed her eyes, flattened her hands on Brooke's belly, and leaned forward, pressing her face between Brooke's breasts. Brooke raked her fingers through Isadora's hair. Isadora gently licked Brooke's left breast and watched her soft, pink nipple grow dark and hard.

Brooke heard herself utter a sharp cry as Isadora's lip lightly brushed her nipple, dabbing it with her tongue. The excruciating pleasure was unbearable. She had never felt so wet, so wanton. Her thighs were soaked.

Brooke pushed Isadora's buttocks down and rubbed against the warmth between Isadora's legs. Brooke was utterly lost in her own pleasure. The rest of the world ceased to exist in the face of her overpowering lust.

Isadora sat up and unstrapped Brooke's belt buckle. Brooke lifted her hips and Isadora slid her jeans and panties over them and down her slim legs. She tossed the clothes to the floor and dipped between Brooke's firm thighs. The feel of Isadora's breath on her skin made her shiver. Her pelvis rose to meet Isadora's tongue.

Isadora explored Brooke slowly, finding the places where the moist skin was a raw nerve. Brooke cried out, a slave to the pleasure Isadora was giving her. Isadora teased and tormented, her tongue flicking, her lips squeezing, her fingers stroking. Each time Isadora's tongue touched her, exquisite jolts of pleasure shook Brooke's body until Isadora's touch didn't stop and the tension built, knotting her muscles in incredible ecstasy. Brooke writhed wildly as she peaked, her hips rising, grabbing for that orgasm.

Brooke huffed like a locomotive as she raced towards the brink… and then her body arched up, quivering, her face shaking, her mouth gaping open in a silent scream of joyous release. She was suspended for a long second, tears streaking from the corners of her eyes. Her body bucked violently once, twice, three times, and then she fell slowly to the cushions.

Brooke was laying there utterly spent, her body flushed and damp with sweat, when she heard Isadora's husky voice. "My turn."

CHAPTER SEVEN

Santa Monica
Saturday, June 15, 10:30 a.m.

"Look at yourself, Mack, you're walking like you have a ten-inch spike up your ass." Sergeant Ronald Shaw sat on a stool inside the Blue Yonder Airways hangar and watched Brett Macklin hobble away from the Cessna that had just taxied in. "You should have stayed in the hospital."

"Fuck you," Macklin said, dumping his duffel bag on the table behind the black detective. Shaw detected none of Macklin's good-natured ribbing in the remark. It was unadulterated animosity.

"Hey, buddy, before you start mouthing off, think about why you aren't rotting in a Mexican prison right now," Shaw said. "I want some cooperation from you, and I—"

"Save it, Ronny," Macklin interrupted. "I appreciate whatever you said to the Mexican authorities, but let's be honest, okay? You did it to save your ass, too. Stocker is scared shitless someone will find out I've killed for the LAPD."

Macklin dragged himself to his office. Without bothering to brush aside the dusty papers and files, Macklin carefully lowered himself onto the torn black vinyl sofa against the far wall. He closed his eyes and imagined the pain he felt as fluid, as a puddle, and visualized it evaporating into the air like the steam from a vaporizer.

Shaw sat on the edge of Macklin's desk and sighed. "You wouldn't be back unless you had something on the killer."

Macklin said nothing.

"What have you got, Mack? Tell me."

Shaw stared down at Macklin. Two long, silent minutes passed between them.

"It's my responsibility now, Mack."

"The Bitch killed Mort. The Bitch is after me."

"Mr. Jury."

"Yeah, Mr. Jury."

Shaw sighed. "I'm going to call Ortega. I'll find out what you know."

"Good. By then it will be over."

"You are such a goddamn hypocrite. What happened to your ridiculous creed? What happened to only killing when the law fails, when the guilty go free?"

"The law is irrelevant," Macklin said. "She'll kill you, my family, and whatever's left of my life." Macklin sat up slowly. "And then she'll slit my throat."

"That's hypothetical bullshit."

"I feel it."

"So sit beside Cory's bed with a shotgun in your lap and let me do my job."

Macklin stood up uneasily, grabbing Shaw's forearm to balance himself. "Don't push me, Ronny. I've got nothing left to lose. Get in my way, and I'll go to the press. Imagine what will happen when the city finds out the LAPD has an assassin on their payroll."

"You can't even stand up on your own," Shaw said. "How can you fight her like this?"

Macklin glared at his friend. "This began with me and it will end with me, one way or the other."

Shaw slid off the desk. "You are one stupid son of a bitch, Mack." He walked out the office door. "I hope you've got a coffin picked out."

❧ ❧ ❧

12:30 p.m.

Surreal. That's what a handful of codeine made Brett Macklin's world—it made it tilt, it made the sunlight a different shade of bright, and it diffused pain into wisps of smoke that fleetingly breezed through his psyche.

The codeine gave him the illusion of health and strength he needed to find the downtown Los Angeles address "Cheshire Davis" listed as home when she came to Puerto Vallarta. That was the morsel of information Macklin brought back from Mexico with him.

He drove downtown expecting to find nothing but a vacant lot. He was almost right. The address was a decaying tenement. The windows on the bottom floor had been broken long ago. Rotted wood planks were nailed haphazardly over the windows. Many of the planks hung loose, barely held in place by a rusted nail or two. Graffiti over graffiti over graffiti painted the building in senseless scribbles.

People still lived in it, though.

He saw some underwear draped over a third-floor windowsill to dry in the sun. One floor below, a man in a tank top sat on the fire escape, nursing a beer and listening to Spanish music from a transistor radio.

Macklin got out of his '59 Cadillac and walked up to the door. It gaped open, inviting him into a hallway of soiled plaster walls and cracked tile floors. The heavy stench of urine, vomit, and booze was palpable; it was like walking through gel. As he pushed himself down the hallway, he could hear the life behind the walls. Starsky and Hutch argued with Huggy Bear. Babies cried. Laughter peaked and ebbed. Angry voices bounced off each other.

He came to the door: 107. Staring at the number, he realized how badly the codeine had fucked him up. *I forgot to go home,* he realized. *I forgot to get a gun.*

Too late now, shithead.

Macklin grasped the doorknob and debated whether to burst in or ease in. Since bursting in would hurt too much, easing in won by default. He slowly pushed open the door. The apartment was completely vacant. The floor was covered with dust. On the opposite wall directly across from him, Macklin saw a strip of computer paper hanging from the point of an exposed nail. Three words were written on it in dot-matrix, computer-generated type. Each letter was a different typestyle and size, as if she had taken each letter from a different newspaper headline. It said:

I'm not easy.

"Damn you." Macklin tore the paper off the wall and jammed it into his pocket. She was the puppet master, and he could feel her pulling his strings. And he hated it.

She's having a ball, Macky boy, and you can't do anything about it.

He could almost feel the strings being jerked on his arms and legs as he left the room and marched down the hallway. *Somehow,* he thought, *there has to be a way to cut myself free, to take some of the control away from her.*

Macklin was so wrapped up in his thoughts that he didn't see the five Bloodhawks until he was already outside. They stood grinning between him and his car. They carried chains and knives lazily at their sides.

He remembered their faces from the gas station.

The one nearest to Macklin sneered, wrinkling the scar that sliced the lunar landscape of his pockmarked left cheek and cut across his thin lips.

"See, motherfucker, it ain't over," Moonface said.

"Yeah," Macklin agreed wearily, yanking off one of the wood planks covering the cracked window to his left. He now had a bat... with four crooked, rusted nails poking out at the end. It didn't send the Bloodhawks scurrying away in fear.

"Fuckface is gonna take us all out with his nasty stick," crooned Moonface sarcastically, pointing his knife at Macklin and grinning at the guy beside him. "I might piss my pants I'm so scared, Rambo."

"Let's see how far we can jam it up fag boy's ass," Rambo replied, swinging his chain and shifting his weight from one to foot to the other.

The whole scene had such a dreamlike quality, thanks to the codeine, the heat, and the Spanish music, that Macklin half thought it wasn't happening. Maybe he was slowly dying in a Puerto Vallarta hospital, lost forever in the endless matinees at the Coma Theater. *What the hell,* Macklin thought, if this was his last dream, he might as well enjoy it.

"Stop talking and do something already," Macklin said. "You're boring me to death."

Moonface lunged, thrusting his knife towards Macklin's gut. Macklin sidestepped and clubbed Moonface's outstretched arm with his stick. The nails plunged deep into Moonface's bare arm. Moonface yelped like a wounded dog. It was a very satisfying sound.

Macklin wrenched the stick free and slammed him in the face with the nail-legs side. Moonface flew backwards, crashing into two of the gang members.

Rambo swung his chain at him. Macklin ducked, side-stepped, and brought the stick down on Rambo's back. The nails smacked into Rambo's flesh with a sickening, moist squish. A surprised, agonized cry escaped from Rambo's throat.

"Don't move. Your friend won't enjoy it," Macklin said to the others.

He held the stick embedded in Rambo's back and jerked it once. Rambo screamed, his arms and legs shaking.

"Think of this as a very short leash," Macklin hissed into Rambo's ear. "We're going for a walk."

He and Rambo shuffled towards the car.

Macklin guided the whimpering gang member with the stick and eyed the others warily as he moved into the street. The four men stood fuming on the sidewalk.

Moonface's smashed nose oozed blood down his face. Little droplets hung off his chin and dripped onto his chest. Moonface was clutching his bleeding arm and glaring furiously at Macklin, who edged towards the driver's side door of his black Cadillac.

Macklin jerked open the door. He let go of the stick, kicked Rambo hard in the butt, and ped into the car, slamming the door shut and locking it. Rambo twitched facedown on the pavement.

Macklin was safe inside the hot, stuffy car. The windows were shatterproof and he had reinforced the chassis to withstand gunfire, flames, and small explosives.

The adrenaline of the fight had diminished the potency of the codeine, and pain squeezed Macklin's body. His deep, hungry breaths, from the anxiety and exertion, swelled his chest and pushed against his broken ribs. Tiny knives stabbed his sides.

He jammed his key into the ignition, twisted it, and pumped the gas. Nothing happened.

Moonface let out a raucous shriek and threw something at Macklin's windshield. It bounced off and rolled on his hood.

The distributor cap.

Moonface pressed his bloody visage against the windshield.

"Scumfucker's not going anywhere," Moonface said. "He's gonna eat his balls right here."

CHAPTER EIGHT

While Moonface and his buddies whipped the Cadillac with their chains, Macklin scrounged around the inside of his car looking for a weapon.

The oppressive heat inside the car was squeezing the sweat out of him, soaking his clothes and bandages in perspiration. The temperature in the car was building up. He knew he'd be pressure-fried if he didn't get out of there soon.

It's a damn funny situation, Macklin thought. I'm inside a tank and yet, utterly defenseless.

The two air-cooled, .50-caliber machine guns mounted under the front headlights couldn't do him much good now, unless Moonface obediently lined up his men in front of the car. Or maybe they would be kind enough to stare into his taillights so he could blind them with the halogen burst lamps.

Some tank.

If he survived this, Macklin promised himself he'd add some lethal, and highly illegal, modifications to this 221-inch Batmobile.

Macklin popped open the glove compartment and found some road maps, some .357 shells, a Bic lighter, a Bruce Springsteen tape, and a first aid kit.

Great, Macklin thought. I'll flick my Bic at them, and while they stumble around blind, I'll hit them over the heads with the Springsteen tape and shove bullets down their throats.

Moonface opened his fly and urinated on Macklin's car.

Christ, Macklin thought, is there anyone who isn't pissing on me?

He climbed over the seat and searched through the clutter that had accumulated on his backseat. Old cartons of food, yellowed newspapers, unreturned videocassettes, flight plans, hangers, small grocery bags, and other assorted garbage covered the seat and the floors.

Under the front seat he found an old, eel-skin shaving bag that he had lost months ago. It was his overnighter kit. He'd had one in his car ever since college. After all, he never knew when he might get lucky.

He unzipped it and found a disposable razor, travel toothbrush, sampler can of aerosol deodorant spray, shaving gel, toothpaste, and wintergreen Binaca breath spray.

Macklin squirted the Binaca in his mouth and tossed the kit on the passenger seat. The Binaca tasted good and gave him a little extra moisture on his dry throat.

"Watch out, faggot's gonna kiss us," said Groove, a purple-Mohawked scumking.

Macklin sat still for a moment and thought. A Bloodhawk jumped on the hood like a monkey. Moonface ran a finger down his bloody arm and wrote the word "FUCKER" in blood on the driver's side window.

Macklin had a plan. He scrambled around the car again, tossing papers aside as if still searching for something useful. In the process, he hid the Bic lighter in his left hand and twisted the flame control with his thumb to its highest setting.

Macklin took the deodorant in his right hand and reached for the door handle.

Moonface stepped back, grinning, fanning his hands towards himself to beckon Macklin. "C'mon out, motherfucker."

He burst out of the car, flicking his Bic lighter and holding it up to the deodorant can as he depressed the spray button.

A tongue of flame lashed out of the spray can and ignited Moonface's blood-soaked shirt. Moonface became a blazing effigy, his horrified screech swallowed by hungry fire.

"You shouldn't play with fire," Macklin scolded Moonface. The three terrified Bloodhawks scattered.

Macklin whirled, spraying white-hot death against the backs of two fleeing Bloodhawks. The fire crawled up the screaming men's backs and turned their heads into flaming wicks. They ran until they were formless lumps of sizzling blackness. The purple-Mohawked scumking escaped around the corner unscathed.

The man who had been listening to Spanish music on the tenement's second-floor fire escape was standing up and applauding.

Macklin stared down at the burning logs of flesh, dropped the deodorant can, and picked the distributor cap off the hood.

It was time to go home.

The dark, age-freckled skin was stretched tight over the eighty-three-year-old man's squat, gnarled frame. He leaned heavily on his pearl-handled cane and stared at Craven, his most trusted aide, through thick, tortoiseshell glasses.

The old man stood at the edge of the cliff and stared out at the sea. He owned every drop of it. He also owned every grain of sand within twenty-five miles of where he now stood. The gray skies and turbulent, heavy tides underscored the unbridled hate Craven saw burning in the old man's eyes.

"Tell me he's suffering," the old man wheezed. "Tell me he's bleeding to death inside."

The misty sea breeze blew into Craven's pale face and fanned his bright red hair. "Yeah, Macklin's hurting."

Vicious guard dogs prowled the property. One of them came up and licked the old man's age-spotted hand. Craven had a remote control in his pocket that, when activated, delivered an electric charge to the collar around each dog's neck. It was perfect for training and for keeping the dogs in line if they ever decided to turn on their masters.

The same collars worked just as effectively with some of Craven's lovers.

The old man turned towards Craven. "Do any of his family or friends still live?"

Craven nodded, staring into the old man's wise, scrutinizing eyes.

The old man faced the sea again. "Then he isn't suffering enough."

4:30 p.m.

Macklin's bedside phone was ringing, but he didn't want to move. The bed was nice and warm, his body was relaxed, and the pain from his wounds was a tolerable ache. His head rested in a snug hollow in the pillow, and the sheets smelled fresh and clean.

He could stay here forever.

But the phone wouldn't let him. Its shrill rings rudely yanked him by the ears, nagging him into motion.

Macklin angrily reached for the phone. The movement raised the sheets. Air rushed under the sheets and destroyed the delicate warmth he had generated during his sleep.

"This better be good," Macklin snapped, lying on his back. His broken ribs, irritated by the sudden movement, throbbed painfully awake.

"Is this Brett Macklin?" a man asked.

"Yeah." He closed his eyes. Maybe he could keep that restful, sleepy feeling from vanishing. Maybe the pain would go back into remission.

"My name is Marc Prine. I'm Jessica Mordente's lawyer."

All vestiges of sleep disappeared and Macklin sat up against the headboard. His ribs complained in sharp bolts of pain. He hadn't noticed Jessica's absence until now. He had been back in LA for only a few hours.

"What is it?"

"Jessica told me if she didn't call me four days after entering the Transformational Awareness Life Church I was to call you," Prine said. "I'm supposed to tell you that she's in trouble. She said you'd know what to do."

Macklin felt the familiar coldness, the rage, wash over him, submerging his emotions and invoking the killer inside him.

Yeah, he knew what to do. "What happens after I get her out?"

"Jessica made plans in case this happened. She selected a deprogrammer and gave her full legal authority in this matter. Take Jessica to her immediately. Her name is Raven Vanowen and she'll be expecting you." Prine gave Macklin Vanowen's Santa Monica address and the location of the TALC compound. "Jessica made me promise not to call the police. You aren't bound by that promise. You can call them. I suggest you do. If you go in there alone, you'll get killed. These people aren't playing games."

"Neither am I." Macklin hung up the phone and slid open the nightstand drawer. He pulled out his father's .357 Magnum and a handful of shells.

9:00 p.m.

Fraser Nebbins stood in front of the den's picture window, staring into the impenetrable desert night. The blackness had swallowed everything. All light, all shape, all motion, had been overcome by darkness. It made Fraser feel like the only life in the cosmos.

He liked the feeling.

That's why he'd moved to the desert. Here, he had a stronger sense of control over his destiny. Here, life was put into perspective. Here, screams were absorbed into the dry earth. Here, he could behead an uncooperative subordinate in broad daylight with impunity. Here, Fraser Nebbins was king.

Nebbins sighed, took a sip of sherry from the goblet cradled in his hands, and turned away from the window. Someone rapped insistently at the door.

"Come in," Nebbins said.

Jessica Mordente stood solemnly in the doorway in a gray T-shirt and sweats, the standard TALC uniform for new recruits. She looked healthy and aware, yet intellectually blank. Behind her, Achmed Sabib beamed enthusiastically, his face dominated by a leering grin. He gave her a slight push, and she obediently glided into the room.

Nebbins swallowed the remainder of his sherry and hit a tiny button on his desk. Two curtains moved across the picture window and collided in the center.

"You've done a remarkable job." Sabib closed the door and approached Mordente. "She's everything you promised she would be."

Nebbins bowed modestly. "I'm simply the best there is, Achmed."

Sabib snapped his fingers. Mordente's pliant body molded against his. She pinned his head in her hands and kissed him, probing his mouth with her tongue.

Nebbins laughed. "I see you've taken the liberty of teaching her a few commands."

Sabib freed himself from her hungry kisses. "I will take many more liberties with her tonight, and, as a token of my appreciation, you may enjoy her as well."

Nebbins smiled and settled into his leather armchair. Mordente's hands fervently groped Sabib's fleshy back.

"May I watch?" Nebbins asked.

"Of course." Sabib jammed his fingers between Mordente's buttocks and squeezed them in his hands. "You may want to raise your selling price once you see what she can do.

"Strip," Sabib ordered her, pushing her away from him.

Mordente peeled off her T-shirt, her unrestrained breasts bouncing free, flung the shirt aside, and quickly stepped out of her sweatpants. She stood before Sabib, naked and vulnerable.

"On your knees," Sabib pointed to the floor.

Mordente dropped to her knees, looking up at him with wet, puppy-dog eyes. Nebbins nodded approvingly. Sabib knew how to handle his women.

"Beg for it," Sabib yelled and winked at Nebbins.

"Fuck me, Master," she moaned, "please, please, take me."

"Master?" Nebbins grinned, arching an eyebrow. Sabib shrugged. "It has a nice ring to it."

Mordente fingered herself with one hand and fondled her breasts with the other. "I will do anything, just fuck me," she whimpered. "I can't live without you inside me. Fuck me now, Master, fuck me." Her eyes closed and her head lolled lazily on her shoulder. "I want you, oh God, how I want you."

Sabib folded his arms across his chest, winked conspiratorially at Nebbins, and gazed down at her reproachfully. "You must earn it."

"Anything, just fuck me," she cried.

He unbuckled his pants and unzipped his fly. "Blow me off."

A tremendous explosion rocked the compound, bathing the room in a flash of light. Nebbins scrambled out of his chair as another, unseen explosion erupted somewhere in the night. The house shook and the floor seemed to sway beneath the stunned, motionless Arab. Mordente, oblivious to the explosions, entwined herself around Sabib's legs and nuzzled his crotch.

Nebbins yanked out the top drawer of his desk and pulled out a Luger. Sabib was about to move when Mordente took him in her mouth. He braced his hands on her shoulders and smiled.

Another thunderous explosion quaked through the house, knocking paintings off the walls and toppling furniture. Outside, Nebbins could hear screams, the roar of an engine, and the clatter of gunfire.

Nebbins jerked his head towards Sabib, was about to suggest they get the hell out, but thought better of it. Sabib wasn't going anywhere. A light blazed through the curtains, illuminating Sabib and Mordente in an unearthly glow. Nebbins squinted through the curtains, trying to figure out what the light was coming from.

He back-stepped away from the window and aimed his Luger at it. The light was growing brighter. Closer. Nebbins heard the furious mechanical roar of it approaching. He fired into the curtains as if some giant monster hid behind them. The curtains billowed as the bullets tore through them.

He kept firing. A black shape hurled from hell tore through the window in a deafening explosion of glass, plaster, and ripped fabric. It splintered through Nebbins' desk and stopped just inches away from him. The settling debris filled the room with a smoky haze.

Sabib pushed Mordente away and confronted the fin-tailed 1959 Cadillac with an expression of astonished rage. Nebbins pumped bullet after bullet into the windshield, and the faceless driver behind it, until his gun jammed empty. The bullets didn't leave a scratch.

Brett Macklin, his .357 Magnum at his side, slowly emerged from the car and crippled Nebbins with a look of blistering hate. Then he saw Sabib, the Arab's penis jutting out obscenely between the Arab's legs. Mordente cowered at Sabib's feet.

"You will die for this," Sabib yelled, jabbing his finger towards Macklin. "I will suck the marrow from your bones."

"Suck on this." Macklin raised his .357 and fired.

The bullet blasted through Sabib's teeth and exploded out the back of his head. Sabib tottered, a glimmer of life still in his blood-splashed eyes. Nebbins scrambled fearfully away. Macklin fired again, bursting Sabib's belly open. The Arab crumpled to the floor and rolled onto his back, his erection sticking out of him like a harpoon.

Macklin whirled around to face Nebbins, but the TALC leader was gone. He lowered his gun and ran over to Mordente, who sat glassy eyed and empty.

"Jessie, you're safe now," Macklin said, jamming his gun in his pants and lifting her up. "I'm going to get you out of here."

He carried her to the car and positioned her in the front seat. Her face was blank. Macklin waved his hand in front of her eyes. Nothing.

"Jessie, what have they done to you?" he whispered sadly. The compound floodlights flashed on, shifting his attention away from Mordente. Glancing in the rearview mirror, he saw dozens of armed TALC guards running towards them through the rubble that littered the compound.

He strapped her in with a seat belt and closed the door.

"We're going home," Macklin said, jerking the car into reverse and pressing the gas pedal. The Cadillac shot out of the room, smashing into two of the TALC guards.

Macklin felt the car lurch as it rolled over the bodies. He flipped the car into forward gear, heard the wet grinding sound as the wheels ground into the flesh, and then sped towards the perimeter wall.

The compound was awash in light and pandemonium. The grounds were swarming with frantic guards. The kids Nebbins had turned into walking zombies marched aimlessly amidst it all.

Macklin weaved through the rubble, swerving to avoid hitting the mindless wanderers, and headed for one of openings he had blasted in the stone wall with dynamite. Bullets bombarded the car like hailstones.

He drove through the rupture, the car bouncing violently over the chunks of rubble from the wall. Once clear of the wall, the Cadillac roared across the dark desert landscape, the bright headlights slicing a path in the mess.

Macklin saw a set of headlights dancing in the rearview mirror. A jeep was pursuing them. He grinned and slowed, letting the jeep gain ground. As the jeep closed, Macklin edged the Cadillac to the right, towards the base of a slate mountain.

Fraser Nebbins stood in the jeep, washing Macklin's car with machine-gun fire.

"Asshole," Macklin hissed, flicking a tiny dashboard switch. Two powerful halogen lamps burst from concealment from beneath the Cadillac's rear grill in a flash of blinding white light.

The driver lost control. The jeep veered wildly to the right and smashed into the mountainside. A sharp thunderclap of flame blew the jeep apart and spit a fireball of twisted metal and jagged slate into the sky. The Cadillac raced away into the night.

Macklin rested his hand on Mordente's knee.

"It's over, Jessie." He searched her eyes for some kind of life, for anything. "I made them pay."

CHAPTER NINE

Midnight

Brett Macklin steered north along the Pacific Coast Highway while unseen, decaying forces exerted themselves all around him. To his right, the sun-baked, wind-whipped Santa Monica cliffside crumbled onto the asphalt. To his left, the ocean chewed away the beach. Above him, a wino pressed himself against the cyclone cage that enclosed one of the concrete pedestrian overpasses.

And somewhere, in the darkness, a killer lurked.

Jessica Mordente was asleep wrapped up in a blanket, her head slumped forward. Her chin bounced against her collarbone from the motion of the car. She reminded him of Cory and the way his daughter fell asleep in the car after a late movie. He gave her hand a gentle squeeze.

Macklin veered the car to the right, off the highway and up Chautauqua Boulevard, which wound up into the Palisades. The homes were set back from the upward-sloping boulevard and nestled among trees that rose and formed a lush, green canopy of intertwining branches above the roadway. Just before Chautauqua melded into the meandering course of Sunset Boulevard, Macklin turned left onto a driveway.

He listened to the sound of twigs and pebbles snapping under his tires as the car slowly approached Raven Vanowen's one-story home. She was still awake. Macklin saw a trail of smoke spiraling out of the brick chimney and light spilling out behind the shuttered living room windows. A sporty red Ferrari was parked in front of the house and gleamed under the glow cast by the porch light.

Macklin parked beside the Ferrari, got out, and walked around to the passenger side of his car. He opened the door and lifted Mordente out.

His ribs cried out in a scream of agony that echoed throughout his weary body. Gritting his teeth against the pain, he nudged the car door shut with his hip and carried Mordente to Vanowen's front door.

Vanowen must have heard Macklin drive up. She opened the door just before he reached it. Her blue eyes were covered by large round glasses and she had curly brown hair that spilled onto her shoulders. She looked snug and warm in her oversize wool sweater.

"Set her on the couch," Vanowen instructed, stepping aside and pointing to the two couches behind her. Macklin walked past her and gently laid Mordente down on the couch closest to the brick hearth, where dying flames crackled in the embers.

Vanowen brushed Macklin aside and leaned over Mordente. Macklin moved back and watched. Vanowen opened Mordente's eye lids and examined her pupils, then yanked off the blanket and scanned her naked body, looking for needle marks.

He turned away, trying to escape the reality of Mordente's inert body and lifeless eyes. *She's as good as dead,* he thought. *I was too late.*

The smell of dry wood permeated the house. The smoke that had been spilling out of the hearth for years had been soaked up by the walls or, more accurately, the books.

The house was a rustic library. Every inch of wall space was covered with books. The book-lined shelves reached up to the ceiling and overflowed with volumes. What the shelves couldn't hold was stacked up in discrete stacks in various corners and crannies of the room.

"You did the right thing by bringing her directly to me," Vanowen said. "I don't think it's too late to help her."

Macklin turned around and faced her. "You mean you can bring her back, break this damn spell or whatever it is?"

Vanowen smiled reassuringly and, placing her hand on Macklin's back, led him to the door. "It's not quite as easy as that. I'm afraid it will take a lot longer to cure her than it did to hurt her. She will never be completely the same."

Macklin opened the door. "When can I see her again?"

"Soon," Vanowen said. "I'll begin treating her tonight." He nodded and walked out. She closed the door behind him.

Vanowen sighed and put a fresh log in the fire. She heard Macklin's car drive away. The flames wrapped themselves around the wood. The dry bark snapped, spitting sparks against the black-charred brick.

She warmed herself by the fire for a few minutes and, when she turned, Mordente was sitting up on the couch.

Mordente's eyes were hypnotically locked on the dancing flames. Vanowen smiled.

"Hello, Jessica," Vanowen ventured softly. Mordente stared into the fireplace.

Vanowen sat down beside Mordente and put her arm around her shoulder. "Say hello, Jessica."

"Hello," Mordente whispered.

"My name is Raven." She kissed Mordente gently on the cheek. "I am your new master."

Sunday, June 16, 11:10 a.m.
Cory pressed the buzzer again and let her finger stay on it this time. She really leaned into it, putting her weight behind her index finger as if that would make the buzzer ring even louder.

If Mom was home, the buzzer should wake her. The buzzer could wake the dead.

"I thought you said you had a key," groaned Jake Henderson impatiently. There were four other girls, waiting to be dropped off at their homes, climbing all over his LTD Brougham, probably ruining the upholstery with greater severity with each passing second. Kids were worse for a car interior than rabid dogs.

"I do," Cory whined just as impatiently. She did have a key. She remembered showing the key chain, which she had made herself in school, to Isadora Van Rijn. How could she have lost it between her apartment and Mr. Henderson's car?

"Well, we can't stand here all day, Cory," Henderson said. "Let's go take the other girls home and come back."

"Wait," Cory protested. She didn't want to have to spend another minute with Mr. Henderson. He was such a goon. "Ms. Shih will let us in."

Cory pressed Ms. Shih's apartment buzzer. A young woman answered and Cory asked to be let in. The lobby door hummed and unlocked.

Henderson pulled it open.

"I can go in myself," Cory said. *He's so dumb.*

"I want to make sure your mom is home," Henderson said. He didn't really give a damn, but he remembered Brett Macklin's call. If Brooke wasn't home, maybe he could unload Cory on Ms. Shih.

Cory rolled her eyes in a theatrical show of frustration and led Henderson to the elevators. The doors slid open and they got in. Cory poked the third-floor button. "Kung Fu Fighting" played on the Muzak top forty.

"It smells like Grey Flannel cologne in here," Henderson said. "You ever notice that?"

Cory rolled her eyes again. Henderson sniffed some more and absently tapped his foot to the music. The elevator stopped and Cory marched to her apartment door.

"Where does Ms. Shih live?" Henderson asked.

"Next door," Cory replied.

"Can you stay with her if your Mom isn't home?"

"Don't ask me." Cory twisted the doorknob on her apartment door and walked in. She stopped, startled, a foot from the doorway.

Sunlight, hot and bright, streamed in through the windows and shone, like a spotlight, on the kitchen and dining room. The dinner dishes were still scattered over the table and the kitchen counters. Scraps of meat had rotted into sickly curls on the plates. The vegetables were black. A strange, furry slick floated on a curdled substance in a bowl. Two empty wineglasses were on the floor beside the couch.

"Mom?" Cory said.

Henderson's face wrinkled against the heavy, oppressive smell of decay as he stepped tentatively into the apartment. He was tempted to sprint back to the elevator for a refreshing sniff of Grey Flannel. Brooke Macklin was definitely the Slob Queen. *Dis-gus-ting.*

"Mom?" Cory headed towards the master bedroom. "Mom?" Henderson, a safe distance away from the dinner table, hiked up on his toes and leaned towards the dishes, examining the crud.

He glanced at the living room and noted the depression of the couch pillows. That's from bodies, he thought, *humping* bodies. He spotted the two wineglasses and smiled. Jake Henderson, PI, had the case solved. Brooke Macklin had a guy over for dinner. They started going at it and got so caught up in it they never stopped. Fucked all weekend.

That's why the decay of modern civilization was overtaking the kitchen.

The little kid was probably gonna walk in on the two of them going at it.

Henderson glanced down the hallway. He saw Cory Macklin standing in the doorway of the master bedroom. He quickly averted his eyes. *Yep, that's it, she's just interrupted "The Orgasm Marathon."* He jammed his hands into his pockets and waited.

It was awfully quiet. Not a voice. No we-were-just-fucking-and-I-was-gonna-come-but-you-walked-in panting. Nothing.

Henderson stole another look down the hallway. Cory was still standing in the doorway, her back to him.

"Hey, Brooke?" Henderson ventured. "I'm going to go now. It was a pleasure having your daughter for the weekend." He took a few steps towards the front door, but when Brooke didn't answer he stopped. "Brooke?"

Hearing nothing, Henderson hesitantly walked towards the bedroom. "Cory, is your mother here?"

Cory didn't answer. Cory didn't move.

"Is she asleep?" Henderson asked.

He came up behind Cory. The bed was neatly made and very empty.

"What going on here, Cory?" Henderson put his hands on her tiny shoulders and felt her shaking. He looked down at her feet and lost control of himself. Something warm rolled down his leg and soaked his pants. His stomach began to heave.

Brooke's decapitated head, grinning and staring up at them with dead eyes, was in the center of a white canvas. Her head was surrounded by chopped up limbs and organs arranged at odd angles. One arm was propped up on its elbow. The hand gave them The Finger. In the bottom right-hand corner of the canvas a name was scrawled in blood.

Picasso.

CHAPTER TEN

Sunday, June 16, 1:47 p.m.

Brett Macklin leaned against his kitchen counter and cradled the telephone receiver between his shoulder and his ear. He dialed his ex-wife's number and waited. Someone picked up the phone.

"Hello?" a male voice answered.

This had happened before. Macklin was used to it. The awkwardness had worn off.

"Hi," he replied, forcing a little extra buoyancy in his voice to show that he wasn't uncomfortable with the situation. He took the receiver in his hand. "I'd like to talk with Cory, if she's back, or Brooke."

"Hold on," the man said.

Macklin heard the phone being passed off to someone else, who took the receiver and said, "I was just about to call you."

Macklin's throat dried up in an instant. He knew what was coming next. He knew a nightmare was about to become reality. In the long second of silence on the line, Macklin heard his own heart thumping. "No," he said.

"Brooke," Shaw began, his voice cracking. Macklin heard his friend struggle to hold back his emotion and regain his voice. "Cory is okay—she's safe."

Shaw hesitated. "Brooke is dead."

Macklin tore the phone off the wall and hurled it at the kitchen window. It burst through the glass and shattered on the porch. Covering his face with his hands, he felt his body shaking.

The Bitch, the fucking cunt killer, had reached down his throat and yanked his guts out.

He slid to a sitting position on the cold tile floor. *The Bitch murdered Brooke.*

It was an unbearable atrocity. To Macklin, Brooke and Cory were sacrosanct. Mr. Jury, the violence, the misery, it was *never* supposed to touch *them!* They were symbols of the happiness he had sacrificed to his vigilance. They were the ideal that he was protecting.

But he had failed. The disease had spread. Brooke was dead.

It was a bad dream that had gone into reruns. Shaw looked out of Brooke's apartment window and watched his friend Brett Macklin run into the building. Shaw felt like Death's personal publicist. He was always calling people on Death's behalf.

I'm terribly sorry, Mr. Smith, but everyone you know and love has been slaughtered by a psychopathic, bloodthirsty maniac. Stop by the station when you get a chance, okay?

How many times had he called Brett Macklin and taken a life away from him?

There wasn't much more death could take from Macklin. First his father, burned alive. Then his lover, blown to bits. Then Mort, the punch line of an obscene and fatal joke.

And now Brooke, cut into pieces.

Shaw wanted to cry, but he was all cried out. His eyes stung and his head ached. He turned away from the window. Lab technicians were scooping the rotten food into evidence bags. Photographers were taking flash pictures of the couch. Weary detectives interviewed Henderson in the kitchen.

The medical examiner carried what was left of Brooke Macklin out of the bedroom. She was slung over his shoulder in a coroner's Glad bag.

Macklin burst into the room just as the coroner walked out. Before Shaw could get to him, Macklin dashed down the hallway to the master bedroom. He stopped cold at the doorway. The white, bloodstained canvas was still on the floor. Someone had drawn where the different appendages and organs had been and written identifications, like "head" or "big toe" or "lung," underneath them.

"Oh God," Macklin muttered hoarsely.

Shaw approached Macklin quietly.

"Did Cory find her?" Macklin turned around slowly.

Shaw nodded. Macklin's face seemed so cold. So evil. So inhuman.

"The woman did this," Shaw said. "She posed as an artist named Isadora Van Rijn."

"Where's Cory?" Macklin asked.

"Next door, at Ms. Shih's apartment," Shaw said. It was hard to even speak. "Stephanie McKimmon, a social worker, is with her."

"Is there somewhere you can take Cory?" Macklin said. "Someplace where she can get help and be safe?"

Shaw nodded.

"It's not safe with me," Macklin said, with an emptiness in his voice that made it sound machine made. "She's not safe with her father."

Macklin slid past Shaw and started to walk away. "Wait," Shaw said.

Macklin stopped.

"Aren't you going to see her?" Shaw asked.

Macklin turned. He started to say something and then cut himself short before the words came out. His gaze met Shaw's. He shook his head no and walked out.

Gallery West was closed on Sunday. Macklin stretched his shirt-sleeve over his fist and smashed his hand through the glass door.

The alarm went off, a shrill clamoring that could be heard all over Westwood Village. He yanked up the door latch and let himself in.

He stormed straight to his ex-wife's desk and began pulling out the drawers, looking for anything that might lead him to Isadora Van Rijn.

The alarm drew a crowd to the Westwood Boulevard gallery from Mrs. Field's Cookies and Funtique, where a video display in the window showed continuous previews of *Molten River of Blood*. The people milled around outside the windows, munching their coco-mac cookies and watching Macklin search the desk.

Macklin found Van Rijn's portfolio in the bottom drawer. He sat back in Brooke's chair and studied the slides with horrified fascination.

There was a painting of a man with his head getting crushed between a woman's legs. There was a faceless man sitting in the backseat of a convertible, waving his hand, the top of his head missing. There was a towering Las Vegas hotel/casino, a hand clawing out for help from underneath its foundation. There was a bespectacled man with a guitar around his neck staring out an airplane window, the shadow of a tombstone falling across his face.

Dozens of paintings, each an enigmatic portrait of death. *Who the hell is this woman?* Macklin asked himself. *Why is she killing the people I love?*

Macklin slipped the portfolio under his arm and strode out of the gallery. He shoved past the people, got into his car, slid into the southbound traffic on Westwood Boulevard, turned right onto Wilshire, and headed towards the ocean.

The light switched to red at the Veteran Avenue intersection, and Macklin stopped. To his left was the giant tombstone that was the Federal Building and to his right, the thousands of gravestones that lined the grassy slopes of the Veterans Administration cemetery.

Macklin tried to sort out the confusing events of the last few days. None of it made sense. Mort meets a woman in Puerto Vallarta and is killed. I go down, she flies up. I arrive and get beaten up. She uses the time to meet Brooke and kill her. I return to LA and then...

Who is she? How does she know who I am? Why did she murder Mort and Brooke? Why doesn't she just kill me?

The Bitch wants you to suffer, Macky boy, she wants to watch you bleed.

The Bitch was making him bleed, all right. There were only three people left in his life—Shaw, Cory, and Jessica. Shaw could take care of himself and Cory was safe with him. Jessie was—

Vanowen!

Macklin stomped on the gas pedal. The Cadillac shot forward into the crossing traffic. Cars spun, screeched, and smashed into each other as the black specter roared untouched across their path.

I'm gonna kill the fucking BITCH!

Cory Macklin walked into Shaw's house like a mechanical doll powered by remote control. Her eyes were wide, lifeless orbs staring into nothingness.

Sunshine, Shaw's white, live-in girlfriend, was wiping away tears from her face and was still sniffling when she met Cory, Shaw, and McKimmon, the juvenile pision social worker, in the entry hall. Sunshine embraced Cory and burst into tears again. Cory stared ahead impassively.

Shaw and McKimmon met each other's gaze. Cory was in shock and not even registering Sunshine's affection.

McKimmon brushed the blond hair out of her eyes and gently tugged at Sunshine. "Why don't you let me take Cory to your bedroom. She needs some rest."

Sunshine reluctantly pulled back and let McKimmon lead Cory away. "Oh God, Ronny, it's so sad."

Shaw wrapped his arms around Sunshine and held her tightly against him. "She's tough, like her father. She'll come through."

She sniffled and buried her face against Shaw's neck. "Will the killer come looking for her?"

"I don't think so," Shaw said. "But I'll have an officer here at all times until we catch her."

"Who is she? Why would she do this?" Sunshine sobbed. Shaw gently smoothed her long brown hair. His reply, the three pathetic words, clogged in his throat.

The Cadillac skidded on the gravel, fishtailing as it ground to a stop in front of Raven Vanowen's house. Brett Macklin came out of the car in a crouch, his .357 Magnum in his hand.

He scrambled low to the house, braced himself flush against the wall, and slid with his back against it towards the door. Tentatively, he reached out to the doorknob and twisted it. The door was locked.

Macklin aimed at the doorknob and fired. The blast splintered the wood and cracked the latch. He slammed his foot against the door. It crashed open and he spun into a crouch, ready to fire.

All he saw were the bookcases. *Where's the Bitch?*

He straightened up and moved cautiously through the doorway into the house. He caught a motion to his left. Macklin whipped around, bringing his gun to bear.

Jessica Mordente stood in the entry hall, her arms behind her back, regarding Macklin with curious eyes. She wore a pair of faded jeans and a sweatshirt.

Macklin relaxed, relief washing over him. The Bitch hadn't gotten her yet. She was alive. "Boy, am I glad to see you," he said. "Where's Vanowen?"

Mordente raised her right hand from behind her back. She held a gun.

"Jessie," Macklin began.

She fired. The white-hot slug tore into Macklin's left shoulder and slammed him back against the bookshelves. Macklin tumbled to the floor. The shelves collapsed and an avalanche of books pummeled him.

Mordente approached him, leveling the gun at his head. Macklin blinked to clear his eyes. "Don't, Jessie," he rasped.

He saw her finger tightening on the trigger and he rolled. She fired. A book fluttered into the air like a bird. Macklin crawled behind the couch and grasped a seat cushion to pull himself up.

"It's me," he yelled. He could feel his blood soaking into his shirt and streaming down his sleeve. "Don't make me shoot."

Mordente aimed. Macklin ducked the same instant the gun blasted. A slug ripped into the cushion and raised a snow of white stuffing.

Macklin popped up and fired. The bullet punched into her forearm. She absorbed the impact as if were just a person nudging her.

She narrowed her eyes and advanced on Macklin. He shuffled backwards, pointing his gun at her.

"Don't," he pleaded.

She didn't hear him. She aimed at his head. Macklin shot her twice, once in each leg. Mordente dropped to her knees, her gunshot going astray and slapping into a ceiling beam.

Tears of pain and sorrow rolled down Macklin's cheeks. He slumped against a bookcase, fighting the dizziness. His whole body felt warm from the blood oozing from his wound.

"Please, Jessie, put down your gun."

He watched her stand up. She seemed oblivious to the bullets in her legs and held her gun steady with both hands. She wasn't human anymore. She was a puppet.

Her finger gently squeezed the trigger.

"No!" Macklin screamed to himself as well as to her.

His .357 spat fire. Mordente shuddered. Her chest burst open, spurting blood and pink flesh. The blood-drenched gun dropped from her lifeless hands.

"Jessie," he cried.

She fell forward like a toppled toy soldier. Maniacal laughter wafted in from outside the house.

"I'm not easy, Macklin!"

He whirled around and saw Vanowen's red Ferrari tearing across the gravel. Macklin stared down at his lover, her body lying in an expanding pool of blood.

Jessie …

He had killed her. Just as he had killed Cheshire, Mort, and Brooke.

Now it was the Bitch's turn to die.

CHAPTER ELEVEN

Macklin's Cadillac skidded onto the street and rushed after Vanowen's speeding Ferrari as it charged down Chautauqua Drive.

A row of cars lined up in the left-hand turn lane. Vanowen sped around them, into oncoming traffic. A station wagon swerved out of her path and smashed into the line of waiting cars. Macklin floored it, tearing left across the highway in the Ferrari's smoky wake.

Vanowen weaved in and out of the southbound traffic. Macklin threaded through the traffic behind her. He blinked his eyes into focus. The warm blood from his gunshot wound was seeping down his stomach and soaking his waistband. His eyes blurred, and Macklin accidentally sideswiped a Toyota. The tiny car veered off the road and skidded safely across a parking lot.

Ahead, the Pacific Coast Highway split apart into Ocean Avenue and the eastbound Santa Monica Freeway. Vanowen roared under the Santa Monica Pier and up onto Ocean Avenue. The Ferrari vaulted into traffic with an ear-splitting left turn in front of the Holiday Inn.

A motor home skidded to a stop, smashing into a Nova and launching it into the air. The car burst through the Holiday Inn's cyclone fence and dropped thirty feet into the swimming pool below. People scattered in blind panic.

Vanowen screeched up Ocean Avenue, Macklin close behind. She made a sharp right-hand turn onto Broadway, straight into the face of oncoming traffic.

The cars on the one-way street veered crazily out of her path. One flew off the street and sailed through the plate-glass entrance to the Santa Monica Place mall. Tables, chow mein, people, shopping bags, potted plants, and Styrofoam shreds bounced off the walls. Another car spun out, coming to rest lengthwise across the street. One, two, then three cars smashed into it.

Macklin stayed with her. He wrenched the wheel around. The Cadillac skidded sideways across the asphalt before the tires grabbed hold. He shot up Broadway just as Vanowen's car, to Macklin's horror, turned left again onto what had once been Third Street.

The street was now a shopping center promenade, closed to traffic. The Ferrari barreled through the crowds of shoppers. Bodies rolled across her hood, glanced off her bumper, and flew into the air. People were screaming and scrambling out of her path in absolute terror.

Vanowen didn't avoid them. She aimed for them.

Macklin weaved madly in her wake, dodging the panicked shoppers and the twisted bodies writhing on the pavement. She crashed through the people like a bowling ball into pins. The Bitch was enjoying the carnage.

Twenty yards up, the Spanish-language cinema was spilling out moviegoers. She closed in on them like a shark.

Macklin leaned on his horn, trying to warn them. It was no use. She plowed through them in an explosion of blood, severed limbs, and tattered clothing. He wrenched his wheel to the right to avoid the fleeing crowd. The Cadillac blasted into the display window of a women's clothing store in a splash of glittering glass shards.

He came speeding out, dresses dragging from the edges of his car. Vanowen bounced onto Santa Monica Boulevard and charged to the left. The people crossing the street never had a chance to flee. She smashed into the wall of pedestrians, crushing them under her tires. Macklin couldn't follow her without running over them, too.

Macklin turned right and raced east on Santa Monica. Ahead, he could see three police cars, sirens wailing, speeding towards him. Vanowen was lost. He'd have to save himself now. He twisted the wheel right again and screeched down Fourth Street, made a sharp left onto Arizona, and then skidded into an alley on his left.

He steered the car into a Santa Monica municipal parking structure and spiraled up onto the fifth floor. No one was parked there. The car jerked to a stop facing the glimmering blue ocean. He could hear the police sirens wailing along the streets below him and sagged against the wheel. Unconsciousness was threatening to overtake him. A liquid sense of nausea and dizziness rode over him in waves.

He had to get help. Macklin opened the car door and weakly draped his leg out. He doubted he'd be able to stand. Grabbing the door for support, Macklin rose from the car. His legs were wobbly and the structure moved under his feet. Walls tilted in his eyes. Leaning on the car, he made his way to the railing overlooking Second Street.

Macklin slid along the rail to the stairwell. There was a pay phone on the wall. He fell back against the wall, found two dimes in his pocket, and slipped them into the phone. Squinting to clear his vision, he punched out Shaw's office number and prayed his friend was there.

Shaw answered. *Thank God.*

"I'm in a Santa Monica parking structure," Macklin sputtered. "I've been shot."

"Don't move," Shaw said.

"Don't worry," Macklin mumbled, sliding down the wall. "I won't."

6:00 p.m.

Patients were stacked like cordwood in the corridors of County-USC Medical Center. The hospital had just gotten its share of the sixty-five people injured in the wild Santa Monica car chase. Doctors and police, grieving families and concerned friends, story-hungry reporters and camera men, were all elbowing each other for space.

Brett Macklin was conveniently lost amid the chaos he had helped to create. Shaw wheeled his unconscious friend on a gurney down a maze of corridors and into the doctors' lounge.

Dr. Ralph "Cheeks" Beddicker stood in the center of the room, holding X-rays up to the ceiling light. "I'm risking my neck for you, Shaw."

"I know," Shaw said, glancing down at his unconscious friend. "Just give me the news, okay?"

Beddicker dropped the X-rays on a dinette table and sighed, patting his swelled stomach nervously. "He'll live. The bullet went clean through. It smacked his collarbone on the way out and took a hunk of flesh out with it. An itsy bit lower and it would have sliced open his subclavian artery and probably collapsed his lung."

"Can you fix him up?" Shaw asked.

Beddicker shrugged. "Sure, I'll just pump him full of antibiotics and sew him up."

"Great, can we do it now, right here?"

"This guy should be checked in," Beddicker said. "He's been shot, for Christ's sake. I already risked a lot just doing the X-rays. You don't expect me to just slap on something in the goddamn lounge, do you?"

Shaw nodded and locked the lounge door. "You owe me, Ralph."

"But this guy's gotta be tucked into a bed for a week or so," Beddicker protested. "His body is a fucking disaster area. You can't just run him through here."

"Just do it," Shaw said. "It's important."

"Shit, Ronny, what is this guy to you?"

Shaw pulled out a plastic chair and slumped into it. "A friend in a lot of trouble."

10:00 p.m.

Brett Macklin had to be stopped, Shaw thought as he drove away from Macklin's home, where he had left his semiconscious friend to sleep things off. Shaw knew it wouldn't be long before Macklin got himself killed. And, if today was any measure, maybe hundreds of others along with him.

If Macklin had called Shaw, told him about Vanowen, maybe she'd be behind bars and there wouldn't be anybody scrubbing the blood off the Santa Monica streets tonight.

But Macklin couldn't think rationally anymore.

Perhaps exposing the whole Mr. Jury lunacy was the only thing left to do. It could save lives, and it was a hell of a lot easier than coming up with more lies. He couldn't cover Macklin's trail, and the corpses that lined it, for much longer. The lies were getting weaker and harder to live with.

Shaw turned right on Rose Street and charged towards the ocean. Macklin isn't thinking. He isn't in control. He isn't obeying any law but his own.

He isn't Brett Macklin anymore. He's a killer.

I'm going to do my job. I'm going to stop them both. I'm going to end this.

Shaw turned left a few blocks shy of the trendy galleries and cafes of Main Street and wound through the narrow neighborhood streets, which were lined with tiny, boxy homes. Shaw neared his home and came to a grim realization. It was time to reclaim his self-respect. It was time to be a cop again, to enforce the laws Macklin had turned into a joke.

He eased the car to a stop in front of his darkened house and slowly emerged from the car. The ache in his joints reminded him how tired he really was. When he closed the door behind him, he saw a shadow dart into the shrubs surrounding the house.

His right hand reached under his jacket for the reassuring weight of his Smith and Wesson. Clutching his gun, he cautiously walked around his car and up the front walk of his house. His heart thumped and he felt an anxious tingle in his throat. Adrenaline fed his muscles and primed them for quick response. All it would take was the muffled *phump* of a silenced gunshot from one of those bushes and his brains would be fertilizing the lawn.

Stay cool. That's the edge. Be cool.

The crackly sound of dry leaves crunching underfoot came from the darkness to his left, beside the garage. He stopped, cocked his gun, and crept towards the sound. The woman was a professional. He had only one chance. Her first shot, he knew, wouldn't miss.

The chilly night air raised goose bumps on his flesh and heightened the uncomfortable tension he felt as he inched around the edge of the garage and into the black shadows.

He couldn't be seen from the street. She could slice his throat and no one would find him until the stench of his rotting corpse was picked up by the wind.

The bush beside him shook. He whirled. Something moved behind him. He turned again, spinning into a crouch and firing. He heard an agonized screech and saw the gun flash spark in a pair of eyes.

"Drop the gun," the woman said behind him.

Shaw heard the sharp click of a gun being cocked behind him. He hesitated.

"Drop it now."

He let the gun slip from his fingers and fall gently onto the grass. The Bitch had won.

"Turn around," she said.

Dogs barked up and down the street. He could hear the angry sounds of awakened neighbors. He turned slowly to face her and the bullets.

The policewoman stood with her legs spread, her LAPD-issue Smith and Wesson braced in both hands and held confidently in front of her. With her curly brown hair and freckled pale face, and her starched blue uniform, she looked ridiculously like a schoolgirl arriving for a costume party.

Shaw exhaled slowly, his shoulders sagging with relief.

She used one hand to pull a flashlight off her belt and shined it at him. "Sergeant Shaw?"

He winced into the light. He felt stupid.

"I'm Officer Barron. I was assigned to watch the house."

She lowered her gun and smiled sheepishly. "Are you okay?"

"Yeah." He looked over his shoulder. A lump of bloody fur twitched on the grass under the white light. A dead cat.

He closed his eyes and pinched the bridge of his nose. A fucking cat.

Monday, June 17, 7:00 a.m.

The house was completely still. The light from the morning sun spilled in through Brett Macklin's bedroom window—along with the last surviving member of the Bloodhawks gang.

Groove slipped into the shadowy room quietly, his eyes glued on Macklin, who slept braced against his backboard, a blanket bunched up over his legs. Macklin's left arm hung limply in a sling. Blood-soaked gauze wound around his chest and a rib brace hugged his midsection.

But Macklin wasn't hurting enough for Groove. When Groove was through, there wouldn't be anything left of Macklin to bandage.

Groove slid a satchel off his shoulder, his tiny eyes never leaving Macklin's impassive face. It was time to scrag this asshole for good. Twice Groove had seen Macklin. Twice Macklin had looked like easy prey. Twice Groove had watched his friends endure agonizing deaths.

He lifted a Molotov cocktail from the satchel and hefted it in his hand. The gasoline sloshed inside the Coke bottle. Groove grinned and ran his forearm across his sweaty brow.

Groove dug his hand into his pocket and pulled out a lighter. He flicked it. The light from the flame danced on the damp skin of Macklin's face. He touched the flame to the rag sticking out of the bottle and grinned again.

"Burn, you fucker," he hissed, tossing the Molotov cocktail. In that same instant, Macklin's eyes flashed open and he squeezed the trigger of the .357 he held under the blanket.

The bullet tore through the blanket and blasted apart the Molotov cocktail. It exploded in midair, igniting Macklin's blanket and splashing a wave of fire over Groove. The Bloodhawk fell screaming against the wall, his body melting into a ball of flame.

Macklin shook his head at Groove's flailing, fire-consumed body. "You never learn."

He casually tossed the burning blanket over him and pulled himself to his feet, his face knotted in pain. Macklin hobbled towards the door, glanced back once at the bedroom, now a chamber of pulsating fire, and then stumbled out, his singed legs smoking.

Wednesday, June 19, noon

Brett Macklin's name was chiseled in the marble tombstone. The fresh dirt underneath it was strewn with cut flowers. The grass surrounding the grave was flat and torn from the dozens of people who had stood mournfully an hour ago and listened to Father Harriman's standard eulogy.

He shifted his gaze from the distant tombstone, squinted up at the blazing afternoon sun and then down at his wristwatch. The crystal was cracked, but he could still see that only an hour had passed since the funeral, since he had crept behind this tree, lifted the binoculars to his bloodshot eyes, and watched his daughter, a hundred yards away, shake with sobs.

Not many men get to see their own funerals.

"This won't work, Mack," said a voice behind him. Macklin turned and saw Shaw approaching quietly, his hands buried deep in the pockets of his black slacks. Right on time. Macklin had called Shaw after escaping from the fire. Shaw made sure Groove's corpse was identified as Brett Macklin.

"If I'm dead, the Bitch will stop," Macklin said. "She'll let down her guard, get careless."

"She's sharp. She won't buy the ruse that you died in that fire." Shaw leaned against the tree and studied Macklin's face. "Even if this works, you aren't going to see Cory again, are you?"

Macklin shook his head. "Everyone I love dies. I want to spare my daughter. The money from our life insurance policies should guarantee her security."

Using the arm that had been in the sling, he put the tiny pair of folding binoculars in his pocket and walked away. The motion hurt bad. The pain was so strong, Macklin had a hard time remembering what life had been like without it. The pain wasn't only physical. His heart had been torn out and buried with the corpses of his loved ones. Mordente's body, jerking against the impact of his gunshots, danced in front of his eyes.

"What can you tell me about the Bitch?" Macklin asked.

Shaw shook his head. It had gone too far already. Giving Macklin any information now was like giving a lunatic a loaded gun.

"Nothing," Shaw said.

Macklin grabbed Shaw roughly by the shoulders, spun him around, slammed him forward against the tree, and jammed his .357 Magnum into Shaw's back. "I've lost everything now. My family. My friends. My daughter. My life. I want the Bitch who did this to me."

The jagged bark tore into Shaw's cheek. Tiny rivulets of blood dripped off his chin. "Go ahead, Mack. Pull the trigger. Go over the edge. You're no better than she is."

Macklin kept Shaw pinned against the tree, removed the detective's gun, and tossed it away. He searched him with his free hand, turning out the pockets and letting Shaw's badge, wallet, and assorted papers fall to the ground.

"C'mon, Mack, admit it. You don't think anymore. You just kill. You've lost yourself to the violence," Shaw said. "You're dead now. Walk away before your bloodlust kills more innocent people."

Macklin found the computer printout in Shaw's inside coat pocket. He shook it to unfold it.

"You ran my description of Vanowen and Cory's description of Van Rijn through Interpol," Macklin said, reading. "You got a match."

Macklin's eyes narrowed and he stepped back from Shaw, though he kept his gun trained on him.

"Demetria Davila," Macklin read slowly. "International assassin. Wanted for murders all over the world. Expert at disguise."

Shaw pushed himself away from the tree, picked up a Kleenex off the lawn, and wiped his bloodied cheek. Macklin eyed Shaw warily.

"She's a sadist. Big surprise," Macklin scanned the printout. "Delights in torture. Loves to kill. Murders are orgasms. Eighty-three gruesome killings have been tied to her. She's paid well. Governments are about the only ones who can afford her."

Macklin rolled up the printout and tossed it at Shaw. "She's a real Girl Scout."

"She's out of your league, Mack. You'll die and take innocent people with you," Shaw said. "I can't let you do that."

"Too bad," Macklin pistol-whipped Shaw across the face, knocking him to the ground, where he lay groaning in semiconsciousness. "You and Cory are all I have left. I'm doing this for you."

Macklin put the .357 under his waistband and walked away.

Macklin flew the chopper down the California coast to La Jolla and the heavily fortified cliffside compound belonging to the man who'd hired the Bitch.

There was only one man who had the money and the motive to curse him with Demetria Davila. After leaving Shaw, Macklin's subconscious had whispered the name to him with sickening clarity ... Justin Threllkiss.

It was Threllkiss who'd covertly financed White Wash, a racist, white supremacist organization. It was White Wash that had convinced Threllkiss' coked-out, sadistic grandson to masquerade as Macklin and massacre blacks as a way to spark a race war. Macklin had destroyed White Wash—and the grandson with it.

But he'd left Threllkiss alive.

Threllkiss had to be the one.

But if Macklin was wrong, it was no loss. Threllkiss was racist scum who deserved to die, a loose end Macklin should have tied up long ago.

The security system at the Threllkiss compound had been built on the concept that if any threat ever came, it would be on foot or on wheels. Nobody expected an air assault.

Who would?

So the high walls, the razor wire, the security cameras, and everything else were rendered laughably pointless if the threat arrived in a helicopter.

And Macklin had arrived.

He buzzed the property, shooting two guards on the rooftop and three more that were walking the grounds, before he landed the chopper on the lawn. Macklin jumped out brandishing two Uzis, one in his right hand, the other slung by a strap over his left shoulder.

Three slavering guard dogs immediately charged towards him. He calmly took a remote control out of his pocket with his left hand and pressed its single button.

The dogs jerked spasmodically in midstride as their collars zapped them into submission.

Macklin knew about Craven's kinky love of electricity as a way to tame man and beast.

It wasn't hard for Macklin, before embarking on his assault, to discover the frequency of the dog collars and adjust his own garage door opener to match it. He didn't want to have to kill a dog ... but he had no qualms about shooting the men on his list.

He released the button and the dogs whimpered away, perhaps assuming that Macklin was one of their masters by virtue of having the God-like power to zap the shit out of them.

A bullet tore into the grass at Macklin's feet. Another grazed his cheek. Macklin kept walking. He felt no fear. He felt no pain. Only hate. He pocketed the remote and gripped an Uzi in each hand.

He fired to his left at a guard crouched behind a bush. The guard's head burst like a piñata. He fired to his right. A guard screamed and tumbled out a second-floor window, splattering like a raindrop on the pavement below and splashing Macklin with warm blood.

He walked on. He was a man with nothing left to lose.

Craven ran out of the house with a shotgun. Macklin shot him in the leg, took the shotgun from him, and batted him across the face with it before tossing it into the bushes. Craven lay whimpering on the ground.

Macklin kicked open the back door and cleared his trail with blazing bullets. The scorching slugs propelled four guards along the shag carpet in a bloody living room ballet. Macklin squinted into the settling debris for any movement. Bullet holes had turned classic oil paintings into confetti. Priceless sculptures were reduced to piles of marble shards.

Macklin sloshed through the gore-soaked carpet and tracked blood, sweat, and brains across the marble entry hall and up the steps of the spiral staircase.

Bullets suddenly tore into the walls, handrails, and steps around him. Macklin quickly dropped down to a squat. His Uzis spat death. Three bodies tumbled down the stairs towards him. He flattened himself against the wall. The bodies rolled past, splattering a red carpet of welcome to the second floor.

He stalked down the hallway to a pair of tall oak doors. A guard whirled out of an adjoining doorway, brandishing a shotgun. Macklin fired his Uzis before the guard squeezed his trigger down. The lead spray spun the guard around. The guard's shotgun blasted wildly into the oak doors. The doors splintered open.

Justin Threllkiss stood in the dissipating cloud of wood shavings and smoke. Several hundred-dollar bills wafted in the air, propelled by the residual force of the shotgun blast. The rosewood desk beside Threllkiss was piled high with stacks of money.

Macklin moved slowly into the room, his Uzis trained on the freckle-skinned magnate. Threllkiss leaned shakily on his pearl-handled cane, his eyes wide behind his tortoiseshell glasses.

"All this"—Threllkiss motioned to pile of cash with his wavering cane—"and more is yours if you let me live."

Macklin shook his head. A hundred-dollar bill floated into the crystal chandelier above him. He walked up to the desk and stabbed at the stacks of money with the muzzle of his Uzi. Hundreds of hundred-dollar bills spilled onto the floor.

"You killed my family," Macklin said.

Threllkiss raised his cane and pointed it at Macklin. "And you killed mine."

A spear shot out of Threllkiss' cane. Macklin jerked out of the way as the spear sliced across his cheek and stabbed into the wall behind his head.

Macklin regained his balance and felt the blood dribbling down his cheek. The spear shaft quivered.

He wiped his cheek with the back of his hand and glanced down at it. Blood dripped between his fingers.

He looked up at Threllkiss.

"Almost," Macklin said. He bashed Threllkiss across the face with the back of his blood-smeared hand.

Threllkiss flew backwards into the pile of money. Thousands of dollars fluttered in the air. Macklin grabbed a handful of money and smothered Threllkiss with it.

The old man jerked and convulsed, trying to free himself from Macklin's suffocating grasp. Gritting his teeth, Macklin pressed down harder, crushing Threllkiss' face under the cold cash. Threllkiss thrashed, kicked, and grabbed, and Macklin felt none of it. His death hold wouldn't budge. The old man flopped like a fish.

Threllkiss' struggles gave way to the convulsing rattle of death. Macklin felt Threllkiss' life shuddering under him. The body jerked once, arched up, and then fell hard into the money.

Macklin released his hold, tossed aside the money in his hand, and stepped back. Threllkiss lay upon the cash, his eyes bulging and his mouth agape, crumbled hundred-dollar bills clogging his throat.

Justin Threllkiss was dead.

But in the blinding hate of revenge, Macklin had forgotten what mattered most—the Bitch was still alive.

Again, Macklin had failed. He had let Threllkiss die before getting something on the cunt who had killed Mort and Brooke, who had plowed over more than sixty innocent people.

Macklin backed out of the room and then dashed down the stairway, leaping over the corpses in his path. He emerged from the house and squinted into black smoke. On the lawn, several yards away, Macklin saw the way to find the Bitch.

Craven lay on the ground, his bloody leg twisted at a grotesque angle underneath him. The snarling dog snapped ferociously at Craven's face. In panic, Craven pressed his remote control. The electric charge coursed through the dog, jolting him, keeping him at bay. Barely.

Macklin came up beside the jerking, howling dog and pointed his Uzi at Craven. "Turn it off."

"He'll kill me!" Craven whined. Macklin squeezed the trigger. The slugs tore pots in the grass around Craven's head.

"Off," Macklin said.

Craven dropped the remote. Macklin crushed it under his boot. The dog lunged for Craven's throat. Craven bashed his fists against the dog's snout. The dog bellowed. Claws dug into Craven's chest. Craven screamed in terror and despair.

Macklin grabbed Sam's collar. The dog's moist fangs hung over Craven's ripe neck. Craven could feel the dog's hot breath on his skin. Sam strained against Macklin's hold, snarling viciously.

"Where's Davila?" Macklin demanded.

"I don't know," Craven whined, trying to slide away from the growling beast, from the wide, inhuman eyes, from the sharp, white fangs.

"You're Alpo." Macklin released the dog and it went for Craven, who screamed again, his arms flailing in a pathetic attempt to grab the dog's snout and keep the snapping jaws away from his neck.

Suddenly the dog reared back and hung suspended over Craven's face. Macklin again held Sam by the collar. Saliva dribbled from the dog's wet mouth onto Craven's wide forehead. Scratches oozed blood on Craven's face and between the tatters that remained of his clothes.

"Demetria Davila." Macklin said.

Craven shook with terror, his eyes locked on Sam's gaping mouth.

"She's going to kill your daughter," Craven huffed. Macklin's face tightened with rage.

The dog growled. Or maybe it was Macklin.

"No," Craven sputtered, reading Macklin's eyes.

Macklin let go of the dog's collar and sprinted back to the chopper. Behind him, Craven's guts flew like pillow stuffing.

CHAPTER TWELVE

"She's at your house. She's going to kill them all." Brett Macklin's words crackled over the radio in Sergeant Ronald Shaw's car.

Shaw called for backup. And, without looking, made a sudden U-turn across Lincoln Boulevard. Cars moving in both directions came to wild, screeching stops. His Plymouth tore down the street, the siren screaming.

He steered madly through the Venice streets, screeching around corners, jumping curbs, charging against oncoming traffic. Cars spun out all around him, clogging up the traffic in his destructive wake.

How could he have left them alone? How could he have been so stupid?

He skidded to a stop outside his house and burst out of his car, gun drawn. He aimed at his front door across the hood of his car. The engine rattled and the car felt hot. The house was still.

Somebody should have peered out the window. Someone should have come running out the front door. Officer Barron should have come out.

It felt bad. Real bad.

Shaw ran in a crouch from the cover of his car and cut a zigzagging path to his front door. He flattened his back against the wall and held his gun up high.

Across the street, Jess and Gladys Furnow pulled back their blinds and waved at Shaw. There was always something interesting happening at the Shaw house.

He took a deep breath and let his free hand drop to the door-knob. His hand twisted the knob open. The door creaked as it swung a few inches into the dark entry hall.

Shaw saw the Furnows looking curiously at him. Up the street, Dave McDonnell, a heavyset magazine editor, proudly waxed his black Porsche and, seeing Shaw, crinkled his face in confusion. If they only knew what evil thrived in their midst. Death, dark and sinister, was now their neighbor.

The detective held out his gun and spun into the door frame, ready to face Davila, in whatever guise. Instead, he faced a living room full of defenseless Levitz furniture.

And Officer Barron.

Her corpse lay sprawled like a lion-skin rug, head propped up on its chin, mouth taped open in a mock growl.

A fireplace poker sticking out of her back nailed her to the floor. Blood seeped into the cracks between the floor tiles.

The sadistic bitch was McKimmon.

Shaw swallowed back the bile and edged around the body. Barron was a fresh kill. Maybe Sunshine and Cory were alive. Maybe. His eyes searched the shadows for the slightest movement; his ears strained for the slightest sound.

Where the fuck is my backup?

He heard a glass break in the kitchen. In the silence of the house, the sound was like a sonic boom. Shaw inched his way across the living room toward the kitchen door. His shirt clung to his damp back and his jacket suddenly felt constricting.

The kitchen door parted a crack.

Inviting.

Shaw narrowed his eyes. His finger tightened on the trigger.

The broken glass, the open door. Bait to a trap.

But Shaw had no choice. He had to take action. The lives of Sunshine and Cory were at stake. The door loomed up, huge and menacing.

Behind it, he knew, hell waited.

He braced himself against the wall near the door hinge. Using his gun barrel, he eased open the door. The slowly widening crack revealed Cory, curled in a corner beside the kitchen table, her shocked eyes locked onto something across the room.

She's alive!

Shaw slowly slipped into the kitchen, his back hugging the door. Cory didn't seem to notice him. He followed her eyes to the opposite wall and straightened up.

Sunshine.

He stopped breathing. The room rolled under his feet and the door silently swung closed.

Sunshine was stabbed to the kitchen wall. Table knives. Forks. Steak knives. Skewers. Butcher knives. They all held her corpse in place.

Demetria Davila leaped out from behind the kitchen door, a gleaming butcher knife held over her head. Shaw spun and fired, blasting a hole in the wall where she had stood. She screamed with devilish glee, her eyes wild, her mouth wide in a delirious grin. He fired again as she buried her butcher knife deep in his chest. The errant slug blasted harmlessly into the ceiling.

Shaw fell backward, the shiny metal blurring in his eyes as she thrust again and again into his chest.

Demetria Davila stood up, her arms covered in Shaw's blood up to her elbows. She tossed back her head in a wild laugh. Cory gripped her face with her hands and screamed until she fainted, her t body falling to one side.

Davila planted her foot on Shaw's quivering stomach and yanked the butcher knife from his chest. It made a moist, sucking sound as it slid out of his convulsing body. Grinning, she stepped through the puddles of blood towards the child.

The house shuddered. Davila froze and heard the unmistakable rumble of helicopter blades churning the air. She dropped the knife, picked up Shaw's gun, and walked into the living room. Through the drapes of the living room window, she could see the dark outline of the chopper landing on the lawn. She smiled and fired. The slugs tore through the drapes and shattered the glass.

Brett Macklin dove out of the chopper, the bullets whizzing dangerously close to him. He rolled across the lawn, popped up in firing stance, and riddled the draped window with gunfire from his Uzi.

Macklin ran forward and leaped through the window. He landed, rolled, and came up in a crouch. Officer Barron stared lifelessly at him.

Outside, the wail of police sirens grew close.

"Killing is an art, Macklin," he heard Davila yell, "an art I've perfected."

He kicked the kitchen door open and burst inside. To his left, Sunshine's corpse stuck to the wall. Shaw twitched in blood at her feet. Macklin turned and saw Cory—covered in blood and crumpled in a heap.

Macklin rushed to her and gently turned her over. There were no wounds. The blood belonged to the others.

She was alive.

Davila was gone.

He left Cory for the police and ran back to his chopper. Neighbors were coming out of their houses. Police cars screeched around the corner. Macklin lifted the chopper into the air as the squad cars converged on Shaw's house.

From the sky, the neighborhood looked like a giant model. Everything was clear—nothing was hidden. Macklin peered down, searching for any sign of the murderous Bitch.

A few doors down from Shaw's house, Macklin saw Dave McDonnell lying facedown on his driveway, tread marks on his back. A mile ahead, Macklin could see McDonnell's black Porsche weaving between cars.

The Bitch.

Macklin ped for her speeding car. She turned sharply, careening into the maze of narrow streets that led to the famed Venice canals. The network of seedy backwaters was all that was left of the tidal flats a turn-of-the-century developer tried to transform into Renaissance Italy.

Macklin could see squad cars closing off the streets in Davila's wake. She was trapped between the cops and the canals.

Or so he thought.

She burst through a picket fence and, to Macklin's sheer horror, charged for the family picnicking on the lawn. The family ran in all directions. He watched helplessly as she plowed over the family and then veered to strike a fleeing child. The kid bounced off her hood, sailed into the canal, and sunk into the morass of sewage.

The Porsche crashed through the fence again and skidded onto the street. Macklin stuck the barrel of his Uzi out the window. Bullets skitted on the asphalt around her car. She whipped around a corner and up onto a sidewalk. Macklin, in impotent rage, saw the carnage that was to come.

She cut a swath of blood through a crowd of beachgoers. Severed limbs spun into the air. The Porsche roared off the sidewalk and into the street. A huge Bekins moving truck suddenly pulled out of a side street. The truck grumbled into her path.

She veered sharply. The car spun. She regained control of the car and barreled across a vacant lot toward the narrow canal. Macklin charged over her, banked, and came around facing her as she picked up speed.

She was racing for the water.

She was going to jump it.

Macklin's eyes burned with fury. A victorious yell escaped from his lips as he bore down on the murderous Bitch.

The Porsche launched into the air above the canal. Macklin flew straight at her.

They smashed together head-on. The sky erupted with a monstrous thunderclap of flame. The helicopter and the Porsche meshed into a pulsating fire cloud that filled the sky and rained jagged, white-hot metal onto the grimy waters.

A helicopter blade spun through air and sliced into the side of the Bekins truck trailer. Trees and bushes along the bank erupted in flames. Windows shattered up and down the canal.

And amidst the steaming debris on the water, a blackened body floated facedown towards the shore.

EPILOGUE

December. Dawn.

The fog rolled in over the water and across the Pacific Coast Highway, slapping against the dry cliff like a wave and washing thickly over the Santa Monica high-rises.

Sergeant Ronald Shaw felt strange being outside. The world didn't seem the same. It probably never would.

He grasped the collar of his trench coat tight around his neck and looked out over the water into the hazy distance. An immense flock of squawking seagulls swirled over the frothy swells. He shivered in his jacket and scolded himself for not wearing heavier clothing.

The surf rode high on the beach, arms of water reaching out for the three or four joggers he saw traversing the shore. *Life goes on.* There were so many other people, so many who were living lives no different now from those they'd led six months ago. It was hard for him to believe.

God, how he wished he was one of them.

Shaw turned and strode down the pier, careful not to stray far from the security of the handrail. He wasn't used to walking yet, and lugging the heavy briefcase in his left hand was taking a lot out of him. Six months of confinement, hospital food, blank walls, and an endless stream of game shows were hard to shake off. So were the nightmares, the horrific, recurring images of Sunshine staring down at him with large, dead eyes.

But at least he had survived.

Shaw breathed deeply, relishing the cool bite in the air. The scent of rubbing alcohol was gloriously absent from the ocean mist. A lone merchant lifted the storm boards from the windows of his fish market and paid no attention to Shaw as he hobbled past. At the end of the pier, the single fisherman was just a misty, solitary shape.

"Hey, got a light?"

The voice startled Shaw. He turned, his heart thumping nervously. A stubble-faced wino grinned toothlessly at him, a cigarette stub hanging from the corner of his mouth.

"Don't smoke," Shaw mumbled, vaguely disappointed and, in an odd way, relieved.

The wino shrugged and shuffled off to bum a light off the fish merchant. Shaw sighed and walked on. His chest ached and his arms felt leaden.

The doctors said he'd be as good as new in a year. *Good as new.*

Shaw fell into a bench at the end of the pier. The fisherman hunched on the rail beside him and cast his line out to the warning buoys several yards out to sea. Waves whipped the pier's aging pilings. The heavy stench of fish hung in the air around the fisherman. Shaw glanced into the man's plastic bucket and saw two scrawny salmon flopping in a few cups of filthy seawater.

Shaw looked up into the fisherman's pale, scarred face and dark, brooding eyes and motioned to the bucket. "Is this good or bad luck?"

The fisherman glanced down at him and then his catch.

"Bad."

Shaw nodded. "Well, it's a nice morning, anyway."

The fisherman shrugged and gently reeled in his line. Shaw glanced over his shoulder and looked down the length of the pier. The wino urinated against the abandoned Sinbad dance hall. A woman in a dirty tank top and faded jeans roller-skated towards them, rolls of fat jiggling on her body as her wheels thudded between the planks.

Shaw faced the sea again. A trawler, anchored offshore, bounced on the water. He stared at it, strangely fascinated. Maybe he'd just do the same thing. Shaw shivered and buried his hands deep in his warm pockets.

The fisherman set down his pole and unscrewed the cap on a metal Thermos. Shaw smelled the tantalizing aroma of fresh, ground coffee, steaming hot. The fisherman seemed to sense this. His lips twisted into a thin smile.

He offered Shaw the plastic cup.

Shaw waved it away. "No, thanks, I—"

The fisherman ignored Shaw's protests and set it on the bench. "I'll drink from the Thermos." As if to prove his point, he took a sip. Shaw smiled and took the cup.

"Thanks."

The fisherman leaned against the wood railing and looked down at Shaw. "You feeling okay?"

Shaw nodded, savoring his sip of coffee. It was a far cry from the sewage the hospital served.

The fisherman nodded and took another sip. "I've been worried about you."

Shaw felt another shiver course through his body. But it wasn't the cold. He met the fisherman's hard gaze. The fisherman gave him a grim smile.

"Mack," Shaw said.

Brett Macklin nodded.

"My God, your face. It's completely different."

Macklin took a seat beside his old friend. "Most of it is steel, plastic, and superglue." He took a drink from his Thermos. The hot steam felt nice on his face. "I looked in the mirror and I saw a stranger. It's the way it should be."

Shaw used his foot to slide the briefcase over to Macklin. "This is from Mayor Stocker."

Macklin didn't look at it. "How much?"

"It's a hundred thousand dollars of the taxpayers' money," Shaw said. "He's buying your silence and the end of your vigilance in this city."

"Okay by me." He tipped the Thermos and swallowed the remainder of his coffee.

Shaw studied his old friend, looking for some sign of familiarity in the strange face. "Where will you go?"

Macklin stood and zipped up his Windbreaker. "Don't know. Wander, I guess." He squinted at the horizon. The rising sun was bleeding slowly into the clouds. "I've got a job to do."

Shaw sighed. "What do you want me to tell Cory when she gets out of the mental hospital?"

"Tell her the truth," Macklin said. "Tell her I'm dead."

He offered his hand to Shaw, who grasped it tightly for a long moment before shaking it. "Good-bye, Mack."

"Take care of yourself, Ronny." Macklin picked up the briefcase, smiled at his friend, and walked away.

Shaw listened to the waves break against the rocky breakwater and watched a lone seagull float gently on the crosswinds. Behind him, he could feel Brett Macklin quietly fading into the fog.

THE END

AFTERWORD

The creation of Brett Macklin—and "Ian Ludlow"—is explained in this essay, published as a "My Turn" column in Newsweek magazine in 1985. Pinnacle Books went out of business before this novel, the fourth in the series, was set to be published.

HOT SEX, GORY VIOLENCE

*How One Student Earns Course
Credit and Pays Tuition*

My name is Ian Ludlow. Well, not really. But that's the name on my four *.357 Vigilante* adventures that Pinnacle Books will publish this spring. Most of the time I'm Lee Goldberg, a mild-mannered UCLA senior majoring in mass communications and trying to spark a writing career at the same time. It's hard work. I haven't quite achieved a balance between my dual identities of college student and hack novelist.

The adventures of Mr. Jury, a vigilante into doing the LAPD's dirty work, are often created in the wee hours of the night, when I should be studying, meeting my freelance-article deadlines, or, better yet, sleeping. More often than not, my nocturnal writing spills over into my classes the next morning. Brutal fistfights, hot sexual encounters, and gory violence are frequently scrawled across my anthropology notes or written amid my professor's insights on Whorf's hypothesis. Students sitting next to me who glance at my lecture notes are shocked to see notations like "Don't move, scumbag, or I'll wallpaper the room with your brains."

I once wrote a pivotal rape scene during one of my legal-communications classes, and I'm sure the girl who sat next to me thought I was a psychopath. During the first half of the lecture, she kept looking with wide eyes from my notes to my face as if my nose were melting onto my binder or something. At the break she disappeared, and I didn't see her again the rest of the quarter.

My professors, though, seem pleased to see me sitting in the back of the classroom writing furiously. I guess they think I'm hanging on their every word. They're wrong.

I've tried to lessen the strain between my conflicting identities by marrying the two. Through the English department, I'm getting academic credit for the books. That amazes my grandpa Cy, who can't believe there's a university crazy enough to reward me for writing "lots of filth." The truth is, it's writing and it's learning, and it's getting me somewhere. Just where, I'm not sure. My grandpa Cy thinks it's going to get me the realization I should join him in the furniture business.

I don't admit to many people that I'm writing books. It sounds so pompous, arrogant, and phony when you say that in Los Angeles. See, everybody in Los Angeles is writing a book or screenplay. Walk into any 7-Eleven, tell the clerk you're an agent or a producer, and he'll whip out a handwritten, 630-page epic he's been keeping under the register for a chance like this.

I do involve my closest friends in the secret world of Ian Ludlow. When I finished writing my first sex scene, I made six copies and passed them around for a critique. I felt like I was distributing pornography. "How do you compliment a sex scene?" a girl I know complained. "It's embarrassing." Another friend rewrote the scene so it sounded like a cross between a beating and extensive surgery.

Among my family and even my friends, I find myself constantly apologizing for what I'm doing. Maybe I wouldn't if I were writing a Larry McMurtry or John Updike book. But I know what this is. This is a black cover with a rugged hero in the forefront, shoving a massive gun into the reader's face. I feign disgust, mutter something about "a guy's got to break in somehow," and quickly change the subject.

But the truth is, it's fun. And since Ian Ludlow is the guy who will take the heat for it, I can let myself relax and enjoy it. I'm building on those childhood hours spent in front of my mom's ancient Smith Corona, banging out hokey tales about superspies and supervillains. My work is still hokey, except now someone is paying me for it. And paying me not badly, either. I can pay for a whole year of college from the advances for the four novels.

The opportunity came my way thanks to Lewis Perdue, a journalism professor who writes those bulky conspiracy thrillers and harbors dreams of being the next Robert Ludlum. I used to read his manuscripts and debate the merits of Lawrence Sanders and Ken Follett. Then, when Pinnacle asked him to do an "urban man's action-adventure series," he passed it on to me. Pretty soon I was buying books like *The Butcher*, *The Executioner*, *The Penetrator*, *The Destroyer*, and *The Terminator* by the armful and flipping through the latest issues of *Soldier of Fortune* and *Gung-Ho*. After a week or two of wading through this, I was ready to spill blood across my home computer screen.

There's a part of me that doesn't like what I'm doing. It lectures me while I'm making some bad guy eat hot lead. It tells me I should be writing a novel about relationships and feelings, about the problems my peers are facing. *I will*, I say to myself, *later. There's plenty of time.*

ABOUT THE AUTHOR

Lee Goldberg is a two-time Edgar Award and two-time Shamus Award nominee and the #1 *New York Times* best-selling author of more than forty novels, including the *Eve Ronin* series, fifteen *Monk* novels, eight *Diagnosis Murder* novels, and five novels co-authored with Janet Evanovich. He has also written and/or produced many TV shows, including *Diagnosis Murder*, *SeaQuest*, and *Monk*, and he is the cocreator of the *Mystery 101* series of Hallmark movies. As an international television consultant, he has advised networks and studios in Canada, France, Germany, Spain, China, Sweden, and the Netherlands on the creation, writing, and production of episodic television series. He's also the founder of the publishing companies Brash Books and Cutting Edge Books. You can find more information about Lee and his work at www.leegoldberg.com.